Also by A. R. Lloyd

Kine

The Boy and the Otter

A. R. Lloyd

Illustrated by Douglas Hall

Holt, Rinehart and Winston

New York

Library of Congress Cataloging in Publication Data

Lloyd, Alan, 1927–
The boy and the otter.
1. Otters—Fiction. I. Title.
PR6062.L57B6 1985   823'.914   84-27965
ISBN: 0-03-004434-0

First American Edition
Printed in the United States of America
1 3 5 7 9 10 8 6 4 2

Illustrations © Douglas Hall 1984

For the lady who likes rivers

THE OTTER (*Lutra lutra*). A furred aquatic mammal common on our waterways until recent times. Now widely endangered, the species suffered a sudden decline in Britain during the years 1957–58, disappearing from much of England, Wales and the Scottish lowlands. Today the call of the otter is as rare as that of the goshawk or spotted crake.

Part One

The Voyage

The cry rang as it had rung before the Ice Ages. It could be heard beside the mill and where the river flowed by the sloping woods. It was a piercing call, reaching Hunter's Hall, skirling where the stream became sluggish on Potman's Level. The sound was primitive. It seemed to rise from the vapours of distant time. Startled, a heron barked and the cat at the ferry raised her hackles. The boy fishing from the jetty looked up suddenly.

There was an eel on his line and he reeled it in. The eel squirmed. Once, no larger than the small blade on the boy's knife, the eel had crossed an ocean to reach the river. Now, a savage-eyed coil, it threshed violently. The boy shoved it in his bag. Mist was thickening, an eerie canopy beneath which the moorhen scurried and fish described circles on the stream's gloss. The boy listened. Again, the whiffling cry came: the otter's call.

Where a great boulder jutted, curling the water in rippling claws, the heron stood at siege in unearthly gloom. On such evenings the spirit of the river matched his brooding watch. Bats hawked noiselessly. Only the fish, as they guzzled, made any sound, and the heron drowsed. The bird stirred.

11

Reeds were swaying, something sloshing through the murk, faring heavily. It came with a bold, measured splash by the near bank, moiling through the reeds so their stems rocked.

There was a halt, another heave. Then the otter was visible, broad head lifted, shedding water, body anchored by webbed fingers and half-submerged. Once more the beast uttered, now springing mallard with rising yelps. At last, swimming to the rock, the otter climbed it and scanned the reach. Eels were running. There was a gleam behind his whiskers, for the fewest mouths at a banquet the more for each, and his call was unanswered. Clouds were gathering. Soon, in breeding dress of silver, the eels would swarm.

Lut, as the boy called the otter, waited greedily. From ponds and ditches they would travel, across dewy meadows, from the brook of the stream's beginning to the deep estuary, eels in hundreds, snaking and slithering. Plunging steeply, he cruised in wait for them. A trout was fanning. It darted upstream. A chub rose to a moth, the fish coppery, the moth a blob on the roof of the otter's swim. He let them go, intent on richer food.

No prey surpassed the eel in the otter's fancy and he prowled with impatience, ears and nose clammed, eye muscles taut in the pressing flood. From his mouth, bubbles of air, released sparingly, floated up to the surface in little strings. He stroked the water. In its arms he was Neptune, a ghost if he wished, or a twirling acrobat. On land he could outrun the boy, but that was trifling. In water he out-manoeuvred the trout and put the pike to flight. Now, at sudden speed, the otter porpoised by the reeds, arched back spuming, refilling with air for a second plunge.

As he sank he saw them greenly in the twilight, pumping rhythmically. They came weirdly; at first a few, then a teeming armada, and, in a trice, the silver monsters were everywhere. He hung in the stream as the host approached. It moved sinuously, impelled by an urge beyond his reckoning. Born thousands of miles west, towards the Indies, the eels had fattened in the river on the fish they killed. Returning to the ocean, they swam compulsively. And, swirling, the otter pounced.

There was a flurry, a stream of bubbles and, two victims

landed, the otter sheered through the tide for another kill. He took the eels to the shelving rock. The stone was ancient, wrenched from the hills in some long-forgotten deluge, rubbed smooth down the ages by the river's cord. Countless otters had used the platform: dog otters had fought there, bitches swum there, and cubs learned their manners there. Just one remained and, jaws crackling, he ate alone.

The boy, leaving the jetty, crept on plimsolled feet past the PRIVATE – KEEP OUT warning and, taking courage from the murk, advanced stealthily. The trident imprint of the heron was in the mud. Nearby, he saw the otter's seals. Woods rose from the bank to the darkened Hall. He was maybe eleven, a lathy urchin, half frightened by the shadows but more of being spotted, and, ducking into the sedges, pressed on squelchily. Then, where the beast's cry had sounded, he stopped and, opening his bag, took the eel from it. Deftly, he tossed it towards the big stone.

'Lut!' His voice was a whisper until, with rising excitement, 'The eels are running. I knew you'd come for the eels. Here, I've brought you a big one.'

Far off, a steer bellowed. The otter stood up on tail and hind legs. In the dusk he looked black, though his coat was grey-brown, the round eyes luminous. Now he glared. Lut was sated. The slime of eel smeared his paws and he had no desire for companionship. But the boy persisted. 'Remember? I tossed you fish when you were small. I'm still your friend. Things are bad –' he eased forward in the sedges '– I heard them talking on the ferry: they said the otters have gone. There's been a crash; a population disaster. I've got to protect you, Lut.'

The otter huffed, a sharp expulsion of air that meant annoyance. He enjoyed his own company and was especially jealous of the Otter Rock. It was a symbol he cherished, not only of his right to the water but of early days, for as a cub it was here he had learned to catch frogs, sample fish from the shoulder and swim submerged. Here, where the green stream danced, he had learned to dive and guddle, know the ever-restless tides – and mistrust humankind.

'I'll watch out for you, Lut. I'll keep tabs on the dredger, on the dogs – on the wall-eyed cur from Hill Farm – and on him from the Hall, nine-fingered Hunter. He'd have our skins soon as spit.' The lad glanced over his shoulder. 'We're on his patch. You've got to be sharp, Lutra – needle sharp.'

The otter scowled. He spoke the language of the wild and turned his back on the boy, who was unintelligible. Left alone, Lut had few complaints. Life was generous, a dozen lairs at his disposal – holts deserted since the 'crash' – and not an otter disputing a score of swims. He had few enemies. He scorned the fox, could lose the farmdog in water, and knew how to vanish when necessary. 'A Prince of Poachers', the locals called him, since he fished where he pleased, and where they, when they ventured, trespassed sheepishly.

A light glowed in the Hall. It cast a thin gleam where a door was opened, then faded, leaving the house in its former gloom. By inky gables an owl turned through the trees, gliding low down a ride towards the riverbank. The otter snuffled. Small birds, barely settled to roost, had begun to shift in thickets, and the animal, listening, heard another sound: the rustle of feet among fallen leaves. Starlings burst from a thorn brake. Flat now on the rock, the otter curled his lip, strong fangs visible.

'Don't forget – ' the boy's reminder was urgent ' – I'm still your friend.'

Startled by the birds, small fish fled the surface, breaking its sheen, and simultaneously the boy and the otter vanished, the first sprinting through the sedges while Lut dived. He left scarcely a ripple. When he came up he was far from the rock, beneath an overhanging bank.

A man stomped from the wood to the water's edge. Grey in the mist, he stood gauntly by the stream, eyes straining, mouth as harsh as an oath. The staff on which he leaned was iron shod; the fist which gripped it, marred by a knotted stump.

Full-bellied, Lut climbed the bank. The sky was brightening, the curving reach gaining clarity. Leaves of willow swam downstream. They could be seen beneath the bridge, and a little beyond it, on hissing rapids. Or becalmed in the

14

pool of the disused mill. From there, in yellow fleets, they progressed beside woods, under dewy oaks, to the rock, then on to the ferry and reedy flats. Here, to a now-crumbling wharf, had come sailing barges in days when wool from the vale had been a major trade.

In damp hedgerows, spiders courted, the webs of over-wrought females moistly glistening. Slowly, with glacial motion, vapours slid from the meadows, until suddenly autumnal daybreak dazzled, sunshine firing the copses, striking billions of globules with diamond brilliance. Lut, in sparkling fettle, galumphed buoyantly.

Romping, the otter tobogganed down the bank, bobbed up in the stream, and climbed the slope again. For a time he played on the slippery chute he made. Birds were singing and pride in his agility transported Lut, his own greatest admirer as he pranced and whirled. Then, tired of clowning, he made for the holt where he meant to sleep.

'Aak!' The heron fished with his offspring. 'Keep away from us, otter. Our beaks are sharp.'

Lut laughed, or so the dark glint in his eyes suggested. Just the same, he kept his distance, for the heron's neck was long, and when it struck, the lean dagger would be aimed at the otter's eye. Harn the heron barked drily. 'Aak! The last of the otters! His line is doomed!'

'Aak!' the young birds cried, staring. They stood hunched like grey statues and shook their heads, for Harn was aged and worldly wise. Sometimes, on sombre sails, he would soar so high his five-foot span was lost to sight, and he would contemplate four counties, the sea to boot. Harn knew of towns and distant cities, and the secrets of the marshland. Harn knew of marsh otters, scattered exiles of the channels, the reedy maze. And of their marsh lord. Sometimes, when day finished, Harn would tell of Fingertaker, the great dog otter whom no other dared challenge. Then the young birds pitied Lut.

'He has no progeny.'

'Dare not face Fingertaker.'

'The Lord of the Survivors.'

'On the great marsh.'

Lut dived with derision.

15

Swirling down, he scattered oaring beetles then surfaced buoyantly. The last mists had departed, the rays of the sun curling drifting leaves. White feathers flecked the bank where a swan had lumbered through herbage. Nearby, a water vole sleeked his vest before washing his face with industrious hands. His beady eyes, almost buried in velvet, glittered. Lut hauled from the water and shook himself.

He was on a small strand, rough with scree and roofed by a scrawny sycamore whose roots, a ravelled trellis, twisted clear of the bank where the water lapped. It was a shady place. Flood erosion had pitted the tree's foundations with holes and crevices. Of these, the largest could be followed briefly by looking into it, then it thwarted the eye with a sudden turn. Of all the holts on the stream it lay closest to the rock and he liked it best.

Shuffling into the darkness, he crawled up through fibrous roots to the dry earthy chamber in the tree's groin. Bracken, dragged there in summer, covered the floor. He scratched it drowsily.

Hunter trained his field glasses on the river, but the day had brought rain and he saw little but scudding water and trembling sedges. Blurred images skipped as he swung the lenses: the mill, the buildings of a farm, the hump of Stone Bridge. Trees intervened and the stream was lost. He muttered. The open window admitted spume which clung to his eyebrows and, damping the glasses, caused him to wipe them at intervals. He did so with a large handkerchief from the cuff of his shapeless tweeds.

The room, barnlike and chilling, dwarfed its furniture – pieces bulky as the oaks of their distant birth. On a vast desk, a mound of papers obscured a faded red inlay, the leather rotting. A great hearth stood deep in dead ashes. Death was conspicuous: the mask of fox, mangily snarling; the leering fish, embalmed in cabinets; trophies of horn and of cloven hoof. In pride of place, heads of otters, ranged like gargoyles on the walls, invested Hunter's study with stuffed ferocity.

Elsewhere, maple-framed prints, blotched with age, showed dogs hounding the creatures; peasants netting, stabbing, impaling them. By Hunter's armoury of shotguns

16

stood otter spears, antiques of the field, their metal tips barbed. Long poles, hooked like gaffs, had been thrust into holts to drag out the beasts.

Until they had vanished. Once, in a fair season, the hunt had claimed fifty kills. But by the end this had slumped to five as the victims disappeared, or formed dwindling groups. Hounds were disbanded and Hunter, bitter and nine-fingered, had retired himself.

He slewed the glasses, searching testily. He was tall, a cadaverous man with down-drawn lips. The lips tightened. Slamming fiercely from the Hall, he marched through damp, neglected grounds towards the ferry. The rain had stopped, but the thrum of water was loud, the river gushing. The sky was mobile, the wherry fretting at her mooring.

Hunter halted by the jetty. 'Where's the boy?' He waved his stick, drawing breath. 'I saw him here, large as life. Where's the damn boy?'

The boatman turned, eyes narrow at first, widening gradually. The lad had bolted like a rabbit. A fall of turf hit the torrent. 'Can't see no boy.' It made a muddy brown swirl and was dispersed by the flood. Clacking, the tide hammered the pier, frothing, tumbling.

'Damn it,' Hunter exploded, 'he was here with you.'

'River's rising.' The boatman sucked his pipe. He was stocky and weathered. 'Come up suddenly.' His gaze went to the flotsam: twigs and dead vegetation, a ruby berry, the relics of a season in streaming lanes. 'Lads come and go – that's no business of mine. I'm not in charge of them.'

'He's after the trout, man – don't you care? He's taking trout from me?' The fish were quickening. Already, small ones, game as bantam cocks, fought the flood towards the gravel-bedded shallows where they would breed. Bigger swimmers, powerful bull trout, loath to forsake their sea diet, waited below the torrent. 'I'll not have poaching. I'll see him off, the young beggar.'

'Small fry, mister.'

'Running wild. One thing leads to the next. He should be in care.'

For a while the boy watched the trout in clear runs above the gravel, their bodies quivering. They looked dull brown as they fanned, but when they shifted, darting at specks of food, they caught the light and their flanks gleamed. The crooning flow and weedy smell of the stream recalled Lut to mind.

'I never poached,' said the youngster, 'I swear. . . .'

'You think I'm gullible!'

But it was true, the boy protested, shouting down from the pier to the boatman who stood in the wherry, 'I never fished Hunter's waters. I'm telling you. . . .'

'You were there.'

'To see the otter. I only went to see the otter. It's true. He was tame when he was small. I don't care what you think, *he* knows the truth of it.'

Neutral, the ferry cat drowsed. Water slapped round the jetty and the man, swilling a bucket, rumbled, 'Try that on Hunter; just you *try* that.' He snickered. The lad was harmless – a truant and a liar, but so, he reflected, were other lads. The boat bobbled and the raucous travel song of rooks, booming down towards the sea fog, drowned his laughter. The great song echoed. For a moment the man sat on the gunwale, then bawling up when it was quieter, 'I weren't born yesterday. An otter's as friendly as a sack o' stoats.'

'You don't know Lut.'

'I've known more otters than you've had hot dinners, lad.'

'Maybe.' The boy's tone was condescending. 'But the others have gone. That's why Lut's so important. The breed's vanishing.'

'Aye – so's ferrymen.' That was true. A few anglers still used the crossing, drank the cider sold at the cottage door. For how much longer? Even the old tree whose fruit produced the beverage creaked and whined beside the lean-to, split by four winds. The boatman kindled his pipe. He sucked reflectively. High above, the heron crossed the river in measured flight, while duck, springing from reedbanks, clipped the tops of woods.

At last the boatman said, spitting, 'You mind Hunter, young fellow. The man's a despot. Just keep yourself where you've a right to be.'

'I need a boat.' The boy eyed the old punt in the rushes. She was filling with leaves, and grass grew from her stern, but she offered prospects. 'With a boat I wouldn't have to set foot on Hunter's banks.' Just float, the lad thought, beneath skirts of willow, around untrod islands, from rock to sedge field, from holt to holt. With a boat he could follow the otter to his farthest swims.

'One day,' the man promised, 'I'll do her up. Then we'll go fishing – really fishing. For the pike at the mill. We'll have a go for him.'

'You'll float her?'

'By and by.'

'When's by and by?'

'Half her boarding is rotten.'

'That could be any time. . . .'

Their words fell fitfully, swept up by the stream in its timeless chant. The moorhen scavenged. Beneath the sycamore, the otter, awakening, blinked sleep from his eyes as he left the holt. For a moment he paused on the stony shelf. On that strand he had first learned to kill an eel. It had squirmed fiercely until Lut's mother had snapped her jaws, and her cubs, quick to copy, had made free with small teeth,

19

growling mightily. Lessons over, they had frisked in the water, the bitch leading them.

Lut scarcely dared recall companionship. Instead, he dipped his head and made the drops fly. The stream was cold. To the east, hard-edged cloud formed a black front. The wind was stiffening and Lut's whiskers tingled. Brown-topped rushes were flinching, beds of nettles, twined with dodder, cowering suddenly. Duckweed scurried on the current. Winter served notice, and the otter, now hungry, climbed towards the pond on Hill Farm. Its barbelled carp took less catching than river trout.

Halfway to the pool, Lut paused, listening. Snipe zigzagged from a ditch; teal sprang powerfully. Flighting east, they threshed into the wind before veering southwards, and Lut heard the crow's warning. 'Beware the dogs!' Across a meadow a fox was homing. The otter turned. The dogs were larger than the fox, tongues gleaming as they galloped, wall-eyed cur and grey collies, the first somewhat ahead as they raced at him. For an instant he faced the onrush, then bolted for the river.

It seemed appallingly distant, a mere rill on the levels. Lut strained urgently. Short legs pounding, he undulated down the hillside, a bounding wave. His lungs were tightening. He could hear a dog gaining, and the crow, looking down from lofted safety, saw the beasts clash and stagger, their fangs displayed. They lurched crazily. Lut glimpsed a lean body, lithe as a snake's, an opaque eye. Then the cur was behind him, spitting otter fur.

Her hold broken, the bitch lunged to renew it, but he was gone, racing grimly through the wind, coat matted and gaping where the dog had bit. To his right, a collie chivvied; to left, a hedge dipped to the bottoms. Swerving, Lut hit the growth where a hare had shaped a run, smashing blindly through the tunnel to rest at the far side, gulping massively. As the dogs squirmed through the hedgerow he doubled back, crept quietly to a culvert and wriggled into it.

A voice was calling. Far off, he heard the farmer's brusque summons – 'Come in, you mad devils!' – and the cur responded, the collies following. Lut relaxed. Fear was short-lived in the otter: wit and fitness had prevailed. He caught his breath. He felt oddly light-headed. A strange weakness was spreading, numbing even apprehension. There was blood in the culvert. It was his own blood. The sensation of dwindling consciousness was new to him.

It was night when the boy returned. The old apple tree by the shed had become a ghoul and the cry of a curlew startled him. The stream ran stealthily. Beside it, black bayonets, the leaves of rushes stood guard as he groped towards the punt. He touched the stern. The low vessel seemed vast, a stranded whale in the gloom. She would not budge. In his mind she had glided, but the hulk was intractable, a dead weight. He kicked the planks. Choking tears of frustration, he reached inside.

His scrabbling fingers brought out mould. The punt was full of it. Leaves in damp loamy layers had decomposed in her. He tossed out a rotting handful. Then more. An owl cried. The boy shivered. The night was cold, the sound chilling, no longer the summer shriek of the little owl but the dirge of his brown woodland cousin, whose winding notes foretold frost. Brown owl skirled when stars were bright, and by the pale incandescence the boy toiled.

He paused, gawping upwards. A spooky throbbing filled the sky and, in ghostly formation, dim legions crossed the galaxies – geese on their long voyage to foreign shores. Something rippled on the stream. 'Lut?' A light flared in the cottage. The lad was under the pier when it died again. 'Are you there?' he called softly. 'She'll move when she's empty. I'll move the old cow.' Water socked, pawing slime-festooned stanchions. He heard no more: just the tide and a corn drier humming on a distant farm.

He went back to the punt. There was a splinter in his hand and his sleeves were begrimed. The job seemed endless, but slowly she grew lighter, began to shift. He heaved oars and a pole aboard. There was a length of fraying painter. He coiled it in the well, beside the anchor then, stowing his fishing tackle, tossed in the buckled tin bowl he planned to use as a baler. The owl was watching. Her savage screech flayed the river. Gritting, the boy inched the vessel towards the bank.

Suddenly her prow was afloat and he rested, puffing. Then

a last heave. He sprawled on the aft deck. With a clap her flat hull hit the current and, rocking, she was launched, his boat sailing! Scrambling midships, the boy poked the bank until land slipped from reach and the ancient craft steadied. Her planks were rotting and moss grew on her decks, but she scarcely twitched. She made music, a gentle gurgle at her beams and the slanting prow. He zipped his anorak. The task had warmed him but the air afloat was raw. Shaping out beyond the jetty, he poled eagerly.

A new world lay before him, the isles and creeks of the otter, hidden haunts of the water, its secret shores. He steered upstream for the rock. Dark shapes of cattle watched from inlets. The moorhen scooted. A fierce elation charged the youngster – rid of forbidden paths, of Hunter's writ, free to glide where he chose, past keepered banks, beside bluffs pocked by rabbits, where crowns of thorn bristled, ivy strung on them. Fences dipped to the water. He saw a hare start, ears couched, running slowly. Past thistles and wan moonlit grasses the punt sailed.

Past fields fringed with lean whippy willows; past osiers and withies until, where the ground rose, the ploughland met farmsteads and great trees, black as Aberdeen Angus steers. Then he was sliding close to timbers, Hunter's coverts, keen-eyed as he punted. The view was fresh, an otter's vision of the reach, and he thrilled to the triumph. 'Lut, she's launched! She's sailing and shipshape! I'm joining you. . . .'

The echo threaded the oak boles but the otter was absent. The Otter Rock was deserted. Only stones, shaped and washed by the current, marked the sycamore strand. No splash of stout rudder, no trail of bubbles. What if something had happened? He banished the notion. The night was Lut's kingdom and the beast would be fishing, most likely at the mill pool. The mill was derelict. Creeper mantled its bastions while great round stones, abandoned like tombs, lay where weeds grew. The sluice was closed. All the same, water trickled with eerie cackles and the paddles creaked. A rat scuttled for cover as the punt approached.

Hitching the painter, the boy crept up through brambles and eyed the slack. The pool was deep. It kept its thoughts to itself and, if the otter was there, he was not evident. 'Lut?' The word trembled on the surface. 'D'you hear? I've brought food. . . .'

The mill groaned. A presentiment of mishap filled the youngster. He felt scared. The owl was silent, the moon's half-turned face covered. Something fell on his shoulder. A man's hand. It was a hand with a finger missing, and grasped him heavily. Wrenching free, he fled gasping through the growth to the tethered boat.

Harn croaked. 'The otter is doomed. The dog bit, and the cur's jaws are powerful. Lut is lost.'

'Lies still,' said Harn's offspring. 'Sleeps the sleep of the dying.'

'Which is deeper than sleep.'

'Falls back, his eyes sightless.'

Lut sprawled in the sedges. By what efforts he did not know, for he had scarcely been conscious, he had crawled to the river. Strength ebbed through his wounds as the herons fished.

'Dies unmourned,' they reflected.

The water vole trembled. The stricken hulk of Lut dwarfed him and he gaped in awe at the otter. A rat slid from the vapours. It slithered forward, snout uplifted, yellow chisels where its lip curled. More followed – three or four – made bold by numbers. Gulls settled. The cast was gathering: the grim votaries of mishap, the scavengers. Slinking closer, they watched the feebly gaping mouth.

'Lut grows limp,' rasped the herons.

'The rats wait.'

'Gulls assemble.'

'The pickers of bones.'

The vole trod water. He hated rats; loathed being described as a water rat. Rats plundered his tunnels. Dismayed, he swam to the Otter Rock, scrambled upwards and, perched on the summit, squeaked protestingly. A strange thing happened. The scavengers fled. The vole goggled. He shrilled again but was hoarse now, disbelieving. In all his life he had frightened nothing. A splash broke the spell. The vole turned and saw the punt glide towards him, the boy poling it.

23

For a while, after the boy discovered Lut, the beast lay motionless. The morning was very quiet. A few wisps of mist hung over red-berried briars and the jumble of dead burdock and thistles above the holt. Viewed from the hills the vale seemed drab and mournful, the stream grey – kindred greys in damp layers from ditch to cloud. In the silence, the moan of water in runnels increased the melancholy. 'Wake up,' breathed the boy. 'You can't die on me.'

Late leaves floated downstream. Where the bank lipped the water, a shadow moved. Curving, it flashed a green and gold broadside, lashing across the swim, just missing the trout which had raced ahead. The shadow circled. Frustrated, the pike retired and the vole, paddling briskly from the rock, returned to the strand where the punt rode the shallows. The creature listened.

'Wake up, Lut, for Pete's sake. . . .'

The voice came dimly to Lut and the otter stirred. He was lying where the boy had heaved the limp body to the punt's well. Starting to rise, the animal lurched and lay still again. His coat stared and his eyes were distant. There was no strength in him. Gone was the acrobat; vanished was the hunter who had tracked fish by their vibrations, and told by instinct where wildfowl hid. Gone was Lut's luck. He was helpless as a cub.

'Take some food,' coaxed the voice. 'It will pick you up.'

A gunshot tossed muffled echoes. Partridge fled the ribbed ploughland. Lut scarcely cared. He was too weak to move, to climb the low wall of his prison, though not to eat, for when the boy produced a fish he swallowed greedily. Wakefulness came and went.

Mostly, in the next few hours, the otter drowsed or took tidbits, tolerating his companion until the boy tried to touch him, then snapping viciously.

'Heck!' The boy, withdrawing, examined his fingers. 'You haven't lost your bad manners.' Then, grinning slowly, 'You four-eyed savage,' he crooned. 'You aren't dying – not our last river otter. There's still a bite in you.' He kept his distance. The injured beast was no plaything. Lut had the length of a spaniel, a weight around two-dozen pounds and his dogteeth were daunting. The boy hefted the pole. 'You're safe in the boat, Lut. Take it easy, we'll mend you gradually.'

He shoved into the stream and Lut, half conscious of the voice, saw boughs drifting above and felt the swing of the punt as the current gripped. The vole had gone. Across the flow, in hunched groups, rats watched wickedly.

The boy heaved. 'Got to sail before the boat's missed. They won't find us downriver. When you're well, we'll explore. Heck, with a boat. . . .'

He shipped the pole, steering smoothly with a paddle. A swan flowed with them while deer browsed on thickets. A bright bird darted. As the woods thinned, fringed with dry rods of nettle and withered willow herb, so the reed banks expanded. They were dun-coloured. In summer, when the tall stems were green, the banks were sonorous. Every breeze raised a chorus. Now there was silence. Brown bents drooped. Rafts swam in eddies, muddy platforms of growth the floods had flattened. Between them, in hustling channels, the stream bore reflections of the urchin and granite skies. It was a hushed stream. Droplets clung to the paddle as if loath to disturb the river. There was, in the utter quietness, that indefinable spell only winter brings.

'We're in luck – the boatman's not on the jetty.' But the cat was, arched and bristling as they passed, spitting down at the otter, who swore at her. Stiff-necked, Lut hissed like a kettle then, where a dredger was working, flinched suddenly. On yellow water they shot past the weed-cluttered shovel of the juggernaut. It reeked of its labours and derv and lubricant. Lutra cursed.

The bank was blackened. Dredging ravaged vegetation, destroying scrub and rushy cover, leaving reaches bare-shouldered until the wounds healed. Still, some thrived on it. Gulls found snacks in the dredgings while Harn, arriving later, would crack the stranded mussels, strewing shells in the sludge, pearl-sides uppermost. The old punt gurgled. Soon the current had freshened and the flats sprawled ahead, the little brick-built wharf crumbling where the tufts of Potman's Level were nosed by sheep. The flow widened. Behind, the woods formed palisades and Hunter's Hall was a blur, a dissolving wraith.

'Look!' The boy gestured forward. Miles of river stretched before them, endless channels wound coastward. Of such the boatman had spoken: their fowl and fish, the reedy jungles, dingles and coves, and concealed creeks. Lagoons, too, where wild geese came whiffling and pochard dunked. Smugglers' footpaths. Snipe and redshank. All, and more, in a land reclaimed from the seas which prowled the marsh wall. 'Look Lut, the marsh!'

The boy straddled the deck, his plimsolls spaced wide.

'There'll be otters – a mate for you somewhere. There's got to be.'

Lut gaped. The voice was gibberish. The boy was dense as a bullock and knew nothing of frontiers, of territorial law or the signs which proclaimed it. Spraint was thick on the bank. The musky otter secretion marked the boundary of Lut's downstream limits. Beyond, lay danger, the realm of taboo – the domain of Fingertaker, whom no otter challenged. But Lut gave up; he was too weary. The other was steering – the doltish chatterer.

A shadow moved, grizzled and watchful, darkly vigilant. Since nightfall Fingertaker had travelled many miles. By

26

Five Watering and Kent Ditch the great otter had passed to Wet Level, a far outpost of his dominion, where he picked up the river. He smelled it now. Jowls quivered fiercely. He was formidable, a giant among otters. And in the gloom his teeth glinted, for on the stream's exhalations the beast scented a rival. The trace was thick. It wafted out from the far bank.

Fingertaker curbed his fury. Another smell made him cautious: a peaty odour borne on smoke across the water from the brick bothy where shepherds once sheltered. For years it had been empty; now a fire burned on the threshold. The old otter held back. For a while he prowled the sedges then lay up in the ruins of a swan's nest, brooding on his anger. In time the flames guttered and, by the pale pre-dawn gleam, he saw the punt leave her moorings and put out on the current.

The great beast stirred. The scars of war striped his sinews. His blunt-nosed head was belligerent. With a snort, he swam the yet dusky stream and examined the tide line. The prints of plimsolls scored the bank, leading up to the hut and a mound of white ashes. Fingertaker sniffed warily. Ends of wood, charred and cold, formed a circle, and there were lumps of scorched mud in which the boy had baked fish. The otter quizzed the dark shelter.

The earthen floor was compressed where a sleeping bag had rested. An empty bean tin offended. But the odours were human and the animal, turning, retraced his steps to the water, nose to the draughts the stream cushioned. He glared. Lut's scent lingered, now inclining downriver. Fingertaker clawed the turf. He shook with anger. In his rage, he kicked divots. The intrusion was brazen and the mighty beast trembled. Battle pulsed in the monster. He stood upright, eyes blazing, invoking past conquests, rivals killed or cast impotent before him in the manner of otter combat, their *pennes* gored. No stranger flouted Fingertaker. No dog otter passed him. He was Lord of the Survivors, scourge of intruders. The marsh was his kingdom.

Men who had glimpsed him put his length, overall, at close on five feet. But he marched with his back humped, like a longbow drawn for action, the powerful neck horizontal. His grey snout quested. Despite his size, the beast stole forth

27

inconspicuously, concealed by wintry herbage or, when he took to the water, with the sparest of signals. At one point he climbed a hummock, surveying the reaches. All he saw was the punt, but his nose was not deceived. Lut was somewhere ahead and the stalker watched.

The boy said, 'Careful, be patient.'

On the boat there was tension, for Lut was now active and restless for freedom, a fretful passenger. Convalescent in the scuppers, he breathed the water, reaching over the beam planks, nervous of plunging. The stream had broadened. Capacious now between the reedbanks, it asked little of a helmsman and, though the vessel was leaky, her condition was stable, maintained by periodic baling. 'Take care.' The boy was anxious for the otter. 'There's plenty of time. I don't want you drowning.'

A breeze was rising. It drove dark clouds up the river. Lut regarded the wavelets. If he could make it to the bank, he might trek home in stages, lying up where there was cover. For a while he wavered on the gunwale, rocking like a seesaw, then – 'Lut!' the exclamation was his trigger and a splash marked his exit.

The boy eyed the ripples. 'I might have known it.' He leaned out from the deck. 'Don't stay under, you numskull. For Pete's sake, where are you?'

A drenched profile broke the surface. The otter bobbed, dazed by his sudden immersion. A dull buzz filled his head, a sullen humming, and he saw it was raining, the downpour droning on the current. Lut dunked playfully. The squall was shaking the sedges, whipping, hustling them. He cart-wheeled underwater, chasing waves as he resurfaced, and a surge of glee swept through the otter. He had lost none of his skill. It was, indeed, the boy who struggled, his troll line snagged, the boat veering.

The voice was fearful. 'Come back. You're not fit yet.'

Lut's view was the contrary. The old braggart was in him and, resolved to show his paces, he searched for quarry. Roach were rising in the slack. They could be foolish. Bloated, in brackish water, they could be taken by a cub, or the boy himself. But here, where the depths were transparent, the fish were not stupid. They were a challenge, a test of his recovery. Diving, Lut spiralled down by muddy bulwarks, skin tingling, back in the flood, the otter's element.

A mere shadow, he sank to the chasm at the stream's belly. Submerged thickets snatched at him. Something skeletal, the ancient wreck of a barge, loomed on the bottom, leeches rising with contractions from its black bones. Molluscs laboured in the silt. A crayfish bolted. The otter skimmed their domain with gliding stealth. Above him, against the surface, the browsing roach showed as dark hulls.

Lut kicked suddenly. Raising his nose, he shot up like a rocket, gushing bubbles, homing on the belly of the nearest fish. He was elated. He was thrilled by the sensation, the rush of water around his body. The fish shifted. With a twist, the otter adjusted vector, his speed increasing. The roach saw nothing. Teeth spanned the scaly girth, unsparing as deep-locking jaws clamped and Lut towered from the river. Rolling over, he juggled his kill in the webbed paws.

'Lut, you can eat it aboard!'

But Lut's dependence had vanished. He had caught his own breakfast and could do as he pleased. Back was the clown, the dashing poacher, playing tricks in the water, dining teasingly ashore, no longer awed by the boy or by the unfamiliar levels. He ate scornfully.

The rain persisted. It oozed through the boy's collar and he sighed, squatting damply amidships. A bottle wallowed past, drifting down beyond the punt, which yawed slowly at anchor. Lut crouched on the bank. 'Are you coming?' the lad called, 'You're not properly fit yet. You need to rest.'

The otter ignored him.

'Don't forget, Lut, we're pals. There are two of us now. You can't push off. . . .' Lut looked first at the boy, and then at the remains of the fish. Snatching a last bite, he lolloped to the flood, paused and sank in the water. The other wailed. 'Not *that* way. Hell's fire, you can't go back when I've got the boat for us. You'll be glad of it soon – you'll be tired again.'

The beast thrust against the current.

'All right.' There was a lump in the boy's throat. 'Go on,' he flung at the small swirl of bubbles. 'All I did was save your life. Don't thank me for nothing. Go on, if you must – if you

29

think you know best. . . .' He watched the wake forge upriver, losing speed in the flow until the rain all but obscured it, then saw it turn, slowly shaping a U, veering back towards the vessel. His beam trembled. 'Come on, Lut.' It was a croak. The boy's cheeks were wet with drizzle. 'Come on, we're travelling together. Come aboard and sleep off what you've eaten.'

He hauled on the anchor. Lut had plopped into the well and curled up in his corner. He snored possessively.

According to marsh lore, the God of Storm had made the waters where life evolved. So ran the legend, and truly Lut, whose line was old when Man awakened, enjoyed a cloud-burst. Now, thrilled by the sound of thunder, he cared little that by noon the banks were gloomy as night, the drenched boat wallowing. The violence enthralled him. He had smelled it coming, primeval in its force, and breathed the sulphurous discharge with avid lungs.

The first lightning had been remote. Far to sea, it had forked on a skyline yet undarkened by storm clouds. Blacker, then, had been vast herds of Brent geese, joined by white-fronts, swirling in from the saltings to feed on cornfields. Puddling the young wheat, they were dispersed by angry farmers so that the flocks had blotched the heavens, perhaps two thousand fowl airborne. Behind, the thunder mounted. The marsh hid none of the drama, its great stage unclut-tered, and as the margins had darkened, the sky grew bloated with vapours of loury majesty.

Lut welcomed the deluge. The rain caressed him, running back from his head by small widely spaced ears and flicking brightly off his guard hairs. But the old punt was filling.

From her deck he watched the pool deepen, soggy tackle floating midships. The boy was baling, a frantic figure in rainproofs. Still Lut marvelled. Lut felt the voltage in his whiskers, the force which veined the gloom with lightning. The storm was power. It filled the river, a paean to creation, the teeming flow.

The boy slipped. The planks were greasy with water. The stuff was sloshing in, encroaching at greater speed than he could shift it. He rolled his eyes at the otter. 'I think she's going, Lut, sinking!'

Lut allowed him a sidelong glance.

'I'll have to put her aground. . . .'

But Lut's interest was fleeting. Beside the storm's fiery grandeur, the boy's antics – heaving oars, baling, scrambling for possessions – were not compelling. Without a further look backwards, the otter slipped from the stern and, resting lightly on the current, simply relished the downpour, feet uppermost. Thunder growled and lightning sheeted. Once in a while a blue bolt would link earth and sky-ceiling, illuminating the cloud cliffs and murky peaks. Lut's mind soared. For a time he forgot the punt. Then, stroking downstream, came upon her again in the swirling gloom.

Almost wholly submerged, the craft floated like a dead donkey, the boy wrestling to turn her from the tide. Eddies clawed as the boat drifted, but she clung stubbornly to her course while Lut cavorted unconcerned. The otter porpoised. Ahead, a ghostly shape spanned the river. Nosing forward, he grew cautious. The bridge was dim in the rain, a puddled track across its ramparts, grey and lonely but, to Lut, a place of possible ambush. He pulled into the reeds to survey the bank.

As he paused, the punt caught up, her master flogging her inshore. Boy and boat lurched in the torrent. Then a muddy spur beckoned, a little cape which would be green in summer, reaching out towards a small osier island – and the craft rammed it squarely, her prow tobogganing. The otter listened. There was a long exhausted sigh before: 'I'm drowned,' the boy uttered, 'and so's the tack. Heck, she'll need doing up.' He heaved on the painter. 'Just look at her. . . .'

The otter made for the bridge. There was a ledge beneath the arch, and the animal explored there. The vault was eerie. At either end the deluge formed a wild curtain, a hissing cascade, but inside the flood was sleek as the otter, running through in silence. The storm echoed. Bits of stone, jarred loose by the thunder, struck the sluice with fluting resonance. 'At least, in here it's not raining.' The boy had followed, his voice ringing grotesquely. 'It'll do till it's over, and I look at that caulking.' He sat down on the shelf.

Lut scouted forward. The smell of spraint was ominous. It marked the ledge with a fresh and musky warning which left no doubt of the danger, but Lut advanced. The time for wavering had gone. There was no turning back and, passing under the bridge, he raised his face to the downpour and issued his challenge. The shrill whistle pierced the deluge. It said, 'I voyage with the storm and submit to no boundaries. Be forthcoming in protest or hold the peace.'

For a while he waited, only the rain responding, posting down long arcades of reeds with its endless thrumming. No creature answered. Yet Lut sensed a presence. The river mumbled. A culvert spluttered, its pulse at one with the otter's heartbeat. He was not alone, he was sure. Easing quietly through the rushes, he was dazzled by lightning and stopped suddenly. In the glare the shape seemed monstrous. The gloom returned and Harn the heron, a hunched figure on stilts, resumed his normal proportions.

The heron swayed in the sedges, head retracted, wings deflecting the rain. His eye was cynical. It had seen many storms – and the bones of many whose destinies touched the marsh.

'Take heed, Lut.' The sky rumbled. 'The old one is near. Be on guard, for Fingertaker is unforgiving and you may yet wish the cur had put an end to your fishing.'

'I have faith, Harn.'

'Faith in what?'

'In what else, Sage of Sages – in poacher's luck!'

'Trouble, son?'

The van had come jolting across the flats to pull up near the bridge. It was mud-spattered, sides veneered with a film

33

of grime through which the letters R-E-M-O-V-A-L-S showed feebly, like the name of a farm on an old gate. The van sat oddly on the levels. Snipe and mallard, disturbed by it, could be seen uneasily shifting where alders marked the landline, and the boy had watched with disquiet as two men left the vehicle – one approaching him. 'Leaky tub, son?' He was wiry, and raw-cheeked beneath the cap. 'Dirty weather for sailing.'

The sky was dull, drained of lustre by the storm, lapwings wheeling in jaded and aimless flocks. 'She opened up in the thunder.' The lad scraped muck from his fingers. He had shoved clay between the planks, reinforcing it with strips of old sacking worked in with his knife. It was crude but the man's grin offended him. 'She'll do,' the boy said brusquely, less convinced than he sounded. 'A bit of caulking is nothing. I've plugged her thoroughly.'

'Yeah.' The remover's smile lingered coldly. He wore a checked lumberjacket and gaitered boots. 'Where are you from?'

'Upriver.'

The boy turned to the boat, too shrewd to be trustful. He had a wild beast's misgivings, precociously chary. The van was filthy. He had watched removers working, and now, stowing his salvaged tack, he ruminated on past impressions. They had not dressed like marsh cowboys, nor had mud caked their transport. He scanned the stream surreptitiously. Lut had swum beneath the bridge and he hoped the otter would stay there, for the boy had no faith in the strangers – in that thin twisted smile or the voice which said, wheedling, 'You'll maybe know Hunter's Hall? They say there are deer there.'

'I know Hunter.'

'Know his keepers?'

'Keepers?' The boy's scorn was spontaneous. 'Heck, who'd work for old Hunter!' He mulled over the thought, frowning. The storm had lambasted its way north, the air was breathless, and the lad watched straggling vapours, vague and diffident, make off beneath a grey unbroken ceiling. He said, 'Hunter's not moving. You're not going to the Hall?'

'Any reason we shouldn't?'

There was a plop.

The boy's gaze flicked to the water.

It was a fish but could as well have been Lut, for the otter had a way of bobbing up to cadge tidbits, and the lad sensed the beast's danger from the strangers. He heaved oars aboard the vessel. His plimsolls puddled the strand. The stream was smooth and he eyed its dun margins hoping not to see ripples, afraid of telltale indications that Lut was returning; but the reeds were inert.

'No reason,' he muttered. 'No reason you shouldn't – nor why you should.'

'You can't tell where we'll go, son. We do removals all over, where the terms meet our liking.' The man laughed, calling out to his mate, who shuffled up with grudging footsteps. 'The boy knows the Hall. He's come from that way.'

The remover's mate grunted. His face was lumpy with blubber. 'Let's eat and get on.' He viewed the boy with indifference. 'We only stopped here to grub. Let's get on with it.'

His partner grinned at the youngster. The grin writhed and jerked like live bait.

The boy forced a snicker. Thought of food made him hungry. His stores had gone in the storm and Lut had cleaned out his fish bag. He stowed his rods. As he did so, his ears caught a rustle and he straightened. The sound came nearer. Looking up, the boy saw starlings drubbing inland, a dense cloud, black wings stabbing the air. Their departure left a vacuum of silence until, 'Keep still!' rasped the fat man. 'Watch the osier island. Watch them foot-rotting reeds. There's an otter among 'em. I saw his whiskers.'

The first remover was crouching.

The boy gazed at the islet. Nothing moved.

'There!' The fat man was running. 'He's away to the far bank. He's hid in the rushes. Let's get over the bridge.'

'Wait!' The boy tried to stop them. 'There's no otters on this river.' But they were scouting now, the big remover's paunch bouncing. 'Please wait. . . .'

'Stay there, son.'

35

'There's no otters. . . .'

But the men had quickened pace and he saw them turn across the bridge to a small clump of willows. Marsh scrub swallowed them. The youngster pondered the van. At least Lut was not stupid; he would shy clear of strangers. The van was tempting. It stood square in the greyness like a large dirty box, a door invitingly open. The boy glanced back. Stealing up to the cab, he peered into it.

Stuff was everywhere.

Between and around the seats were flattened cigarette ends, a folded map, cartridge belts, a couple of guns, boxes of rifle and twelve-bore ammunition, snare wires, empty beer cans, two flashlamps and a bag of provisions. The bag held thermos flasks and field rations. The boy drew back. Then, curious, he slipped to the rear of the van, where the doors were shut.

The latch was above his reach. Jumping, he failed to grasp the handle. For a while he stood away breathing deeply, unsure he wished to bother. He knew enough about the strangers. Yet the urge to pry goaded him, and now a running leap made it, bolt sliding as the boy tumbled backwards. The doors swung slowly. A head lolled from the interior. Its eyes fixed him like moons, bright but cold as the carcass. Behind the corpse of the deer he saw gamebirds, blood fresh at the beak, and great mounds of dead wildfowl, duck, geese – more carnage than the urchin could fathom.

He turned to run. Fear impelled him, and loathing, but foresight prevailed. Returning to the cab, he snatched the bag of provisions. *Then* he ran. With all his speed he flew back to the river, tossed the food in the punt and strained sinew to launch her. He could hear them. Their sounds carried in the stillness. He heaved until the boat slithered, then, afloat, slowly swung athwart the current. At last the boy turned the prow and, with quickening momentum, shot through the bridge to banks so soggy none but the webbed or finned could follow.

He called the otter. 'Lut? Keep your head down and follow.' There was sweat on his forehead.

Far behind came a howl – the threat was blasphemous.

* * *

36

Lut heard none of it. Upset by the removers, he had vanished, swimming deep with the flow until the banks were deserted. He could with ease have remained submerged for five minutes, but chose to rise beyond the next bend in the river. There, some way below the bridge, he mooched lazily. The shores were swampy. A few ewes browsed the grasses. Nearby were sallows and clumps of tufty rushes. Underwater the bed was sludgy, and for a while Lut amused himself turning stones in search of eels.

Growing bored, he nosed up to clearer levels. Now the stream was pellucid, ochrous green, and he could see well ahead. A shadow hung in the distance, too large for a fish, and drawing closer he made out bubbles rising, a fine thread as of air from an otter's pelt. Tracking, he could see the silver of bib, a long neck and the effortless movements, graceful and languorous. The creature was maybe two thirds his own size, a female – the first Lut had met since cubhood.

Then the small bitch was gone.

Amazed, he stared at empty water. She had streaked to the sedges, where he found her in ambush. Her eyes challenged him. Quickly dry, she was handsome, her coat plush and silky. But her growl was less pleasing, and Lut, leaving the river, crouched low as he faced her. Neither moved for a minute, then the male sidled nearer.

She answered violently. Growling and spitting, the little otter attacked him, forcing him backwards. He retreated, still dumbfounded. Perplexed, he suffered her meekly, surprised by his own forbearance until, her onslaught abating, she stood off and glared. Again they faced one another. Now her mood was less hostile. She had issued a warning, and when next Lut moved forward, her rebuttal was playful, a boisterous frolic in which the neckholds, like the snapping and skin tugging, were no more than mock warfare.

Squealing, they rolled and wrestled. It was a long game. Now, with sudden abandon, they would race into the water, romping and chasing, then halt in the shallows and spar like boxers before chasing again. In the depths they were torpedoes. Through swirling forests and green-shadowed glades they sped recklessly, spraying water as they surfaced. Lut showed off. He was mad as a jack hare, wild-eyed, and when eventually they rested he drowsed like a puppy. He stirred abruptly. The bitch had gone.

She had left while he slumbered, slipping back to the marshes. 'To the old one!' Lut reproached himself fiercely.

'Hey, Lut!' The punt slid round the rushes. 'Come on, we're fully provisioned. Let's find this mate for you. . . .'

For two days, moving with cautious familiarity, the bitch otter crossed the marsh. Her course was easting, parallel with foaming breakers, picked from a web of dykes and channels which sprawled across the flats. To the north, now miles inland, the ancient coastline rose steeply, sheep tucked in its dingles. There, Romans had sailed, Saxons landed, before great storms threw up spits against which the seas faltered and, fuming, had surrendered the morass.

Here marshmen had laboured, and rivermen. Thomas Becket, archbishop, had sent monks to drain the quagmire. Digging dykes, they had formed the first plots of inned or reclaimed land, raising churches in thanksgiving. Their little temples, grey and lonely, still stood beside the ditches, isolated as the farmsteads and starved of congregations. Now the otter passed around them. Swans grazed in rushy graveyards. Runnels whimpered. By sluice and rill she moved briskly, sometimes swimming, sometimes clambering floodbanks, seldom far from the reeds which stitched the patchwork of innings and formed her best cover.

Once, on the journey, she slept, lying up in tall bent grass; and once fished a pool where bogbean would flower in summer. The small bitch did not dawdle. Plunging into the shallow basin, she twirled twice at its centre, stampeding its finned tenants to the edges. Their size was modest but she took them in quick succession, ate with scarcely a pause, and resumed her trek. Few creatures were conspicuous. A pair of terns dipped to scold her as they hunted a channel. Near a tide gate, the dark ferretlike mink eyed her balefully.

The beast slid behind the brickwork and, rearing up as she approached, took a closer look, brown nose puckering, then withdrew as she passed. To the ubiquitous mink, now at home on the marshes, the few otters surviving were its last more powerful rivals. Safely distanced now, it swore. But if the bitch heard she scorned it, once more in the water, pressing on through the sedges. As she trekked she thought of Lut. She ought not to have strayed, leading on the new-comer, for only trouble lay that way. In the realm of the old one, the young male had dangers enough to face.

At last, another day dawning, she reached the wooded mound. Once an island, it stood up like a beacon from the marsh, its tall beeches crowned with herons' nests, empty but soon to be claimed again. Every year the birds returned, winging home from their wanderings on tilting sails. The small otter gazed upwards. By St Valentine's tide they would be mustering. She would watch their ritual of reunion, its trancelike shuffling. And from her holt on the brook, hear the yelping guard-changing in the high boughs. The scene was old – old by the time of Domesday, whose scribes knew the heronry – and its age pleased the otter. It was comforting.

Here was her refuge, her retreat from Fingertaker, Lord of Survivors, and from the marsh winds. A pink sky signalled frost. The bitch scurried. When the marsh froze, blood and sap turned to ice, since the sanctuaries were few, and she was glad to be back. It was not the river. The boggy brook was a mere trickle, but the place was her own. Soon the returning herons would ease her solitude.

The boatman, watching the rats retreat, noted their inso-lence. They openly slouched along the bank, and he thought they had got worse, more numerous, immune to his poison

40

bait. The temperature was dropping and the cold would make them bolder. He rolled on through Hunter's gates, his breath misting. Age bent his stocky figure. He felt the winds and frosts nowadays, stamping down as he marched to keep warm. At the Hall he called urgently, 'Hey, there!'

He thumped the iron-studded door. 'Come on, you beggar.' Then, unanswered, he stomped past chill mullioned windows to the building's back regions. There, in a morgue of a courtyard, he called again. The yard was desolate. Downpipes slanted and the walls were green with dampness. Soon, he thought, it would snow. For a moment, by an outhouse, a woman paused with a mop and pail before, wrapped shabbily, she cycled off, as beyond recall as the heyday of Hunter's Hall.

The boatman circled the mansion. The grounds were neglected, kennels empty. Foothills of wintry rhododendrons banked darkly to the woods and, in their shadows, the man regained the front aspect, once more hammering on the door. 'Come on, you deaf beggar.' He heard the bark of a dog. The door creaked and Hunter, standing gaunt on the threshold, said, 'Damn it, you'll wake the dead before you've finished.'

'It's the boy.' The boatman breathed on his fingers. 'The lad you were seeking.'

'Well?'

'He's gone.'

'Get inside, man. It's bitter.'

'He's cast off.' The vast lobby was cheerless. 'The little beggar's cast off.' The place was no warmer than outside, Hunter's frame bulked in woollens frayed and sombre as his jacket. The thin face was hoary. 'None too soon,' he said fiercely. Great beams soared above him and the tiled floor was naked. Walls bristled with antlers. The heads were tawdry, thick with the dust of seasons. The boatman thought of his cottage, its fuggy cosiness. It beat him how Hunter lived in such conditions. He glowered around, saying darkly, 'Aye, cast into the wild, the punt along with the beggar.'

'Stolen a boat?'

'Never mind what he's stolen.' The boatman growled his

41

impatience. 'You'd hang a child for a rabbit. Times have changed.' Once the woods had crawled with keepers; you could not move for estate staff. Then, the house had been spanking. Then the punt had gleamed with care and Hunter's guests had fished from her, hampers bulging beside them, or harried the otter. On high days half the vale had thronged the banks of the Hall while hounds drew the sedges. But no more. That was over. Now the place was a grave, the boatman reckoned; its master a scarecrow. Times had changed.

Hunter snarled, 'Damn the scoundrel.'

'Pray the beggar's alive.' Half the old punt was rotten; the boy could drown on the marshes. Or freeze. 'I've got my boat waiting.'

'Let it wait.'

'We can't wait.'

'D'you think I've nothing to do?' Hunter limped to the study.

'There's only us, Hunter.'

A fire was burning and a dog lay beside it, rough coated, flews pendulous. The old hound was snoring but little warmth reached the boatman. A fusty rawness enwrapped him, reached from drab walls and ceiling. The eyes of dead beasts were staring. Hunter's hooded orbs watched him. Times had changed, the recluse would have conceded, needing none to remind him, least of all the damned boatman. Blast the peasant! A crow shadowed the window. Hunter stared at the river.

He said, 'Boats are your business. If you're going, get off. I'm not needed.'

'Not for much.' The boatman leered at his neighbour. He eyed the hound and the trophies. At length he said, 'Save for one thing: to hunt us an otter. There you've got me, I grant, for you're the man with the knack. Always could find an otter; had a nose for their movements. And I'd say you'd still got it. I'd say you'd follow an otter as true as that dog would – else I wouldn't be here.'

'Hunt an otter?'

'Else,' the boatman said evilly, 'you could rot in this morgue; I'd not need you.'

'What otter?'

'The boy's got an otter.'

Outside, the earth hardened, first hints of snow drifting. Far off, the dredger hammered. The boatman listened. He believed the mechanic. The man had been certain – had seen clear into the punt as it passed him. He could have touched them, he promised: boy and otter, the beast curled up like a tabby. The boatman believed him.

The boy had talked of an otter. Perhaps he did sometimes lie but he was more than just a liar, more than a truant and a boat thief; something wilder, more at one with the river. A water urchin. And the water could claim him. 'If we don't move quick, mister . . . unless we know the right channels. An old punt leaves no spoor but an otter leaves tracks, marks the trail for him who knows what to look for. Bring the hound. But for God's sake come quickly – that, or swallow your conscience.'

'It's hopeless.'

'For you, Hunter?'

'Man, it's freezing.'

'The lad's out there.'

Hunter moved to the sideboard. He rummaged massive decanters. They held only the stains of their former contents and he grasped a cheap bottle, filling two cut-glass goblets. One he thrust at the boatman. 'Take it. You're an insolent beggar but you know the damned river. I'll have a look. Drink the stuff first; you'll need it. It skins the mouth but it warms you. By God, you'll need warming.' He rubbed the stump of his lost finger. Hunter grimaced. He said with barbarous pleasure, 'You'll see – otter hunting in this weather! Drink, then do as I tell you. . . .'

'Don't pull rank on me, Hunter.'

'Who's master of hounds here?'

'Ye unrepenting tyrant!'

A white flurry blurred their shapes as they made for the jetty, the fine precipitation forming drifts in ruts and hollows, daubing streaks on the valley. Across the stream a homing vixen flicked her head as she trotted, shaking ice from her whiskers, her rich red coat fluffed for warmth. The coat went

43

slim. Ears pricked, she stood listening. She heard the drone of the outboard. Then she was off, away with a skip through the covert. By a stile, she glanced back. The drone was muffled. The tumbling flakes had grown feathery.

Three herons crossed the marshes. The stream was now ice-bound, its banks snowy, the inlets filled with wind-scolloped drifts. The flats dazzled in their whiteness. The herons flew in wide formation. From below, they looked spectral, cloud-grey wings against heron-grey cloud deceptively languid, flapping twice to the second. No other save the stork beat so slowly, yet the birds did not idle. Veering south for the saltings, they were making maybe thirty miles an hour, heads drawn back, one leg tucked on another, as if snoozing in transit. Periodically, in laconic conversation, the herons yelped.

'See,' cried Harn, 'where the boy's boat is stranded.'

'The boy has headed for shelter.'

'Gone in search of a farmstead.'

'The boy's kind are feeble.'

'Quickly frozen,' Harn granted. 'The boy must shelter or perish. Lut is stronger. Lut will not leave the ice. The otter sports amid snowdrifts.'

'A braggart.'

'Until the old one arrives.'

'Then the sport will be bloody.'

'Then the snow will be red.'

'And the boy's return anguished.'

'If indeed,' Harn's bark ran the ice alleys, 'the boy survives to return, for shelter is scarce, the place desolate. The boy's wit is not the heron's. Nor,' said Harn, 'is he guided by Harn, who knows the marsh in all seasons and is wise above the wisest.'

Lut watched them fly over. The boy had left with reluctance, eyes weeping in the cold, his feet beyond feeling. Hands freezing, he had made the otter a rough holt in the punt, piling rushes across it, then tipped up the food bag. 'Half a pie! It's all I can leave. I'll be quick. Honest, Lut, back before you know it. With provisions, I promise.'

Undismayed, the beast had gambolled. Warm in his

dense damp-proof jacket, Lut slid and rolled on the snow, snapping reeds as he rollicked. Their stems were brittle. Chinking, the pieces whirled on the ice and he skittered after them. Bored at length, he found a flaw in the ice-seam and forced his way under. Bubbles rose beneath the casing. Several times he scoured the free-running depths, returning to the blowhole, at last with contentment, the fish struggling in his grip.

Lut ate and cleaned his paws. He sniffed the punt. For a while he pondered the steely landscape. It was a wilderness. Nothing moved – nothing more than a tiny long-tailed mouse in search of refuge. Baffled, the speck of brown fur ploughed the snowy plain. Lut yawned. If he pined, now alone, it was not for the boy, but for the lithe and teasing female whose fleeting presence still haunted him. On the off chance, he made his way down the river in hope of finding her.

The cold air was torpid. Before long the ice was rumbling. The tide had turned and, now ebbing, unlocked the stream from its ceiling of crystal which, unsupported, groaned then cracked with sharp volleys. In jagged slabs the ice reared, sliding back, nudged and wrenched by the current until the whole was in turmoil. Only the reeds retained a lofted white platform. Lut, breaking it rudely, breasted out on the flood where he best liked to travel.

As he swam, the flow widened, increasingly brackish. The salty taste was unfamiliar. He saw no signs of the bitch, but gulls appeared in mounting numbers, and fowl strange to his experience: shags and cormorants. They flew off low as he approached, dusky witches, long and spearing. Diving, Lut accelerated. Slabs of ice were revolving, turning turtle around him. A shoal of fry gleamed and vanished. The banks had gone. No longer flanked by reeds and sedges, the otter passed foreign objects, dinghy moorings, the beamy hulls of small trawlers. Crinkly kelp swam in the water, unrelated to the weeds of the river. Rocks loomed to the surface. Scrambling up them, Lut perched on the summit.

He had seen nothing like it. To his front, as far as sight travelled, a heaving grey expanse met his gaze, a vast cradle of shadows rocking under the cloud grid. Lut looked at the sea. For the first time in his life, water awed him. He marvelled at the vision. And as he did, the clouds parted, soared asunder, pouring sunlight on the rollers, replacing their dullness with silvery brilliance. The otter wriggled. The urge to plunge overwhelmed him. Snarling combers were pounding. Spume flew as they exploded, their undertow rattling. The boom and hiss thrilled the animal.

Revelling, he hurled himself at the breakers. It was sport beyond excellence. The waves intoxicated him. Lut stove through their walls, dived and surfed as they thundered. There was no end to their exuberance. Now engulfed in briny torrents, now riding the foam crests, now bobbing in troughs, looping, arrowing, the otter disported. Exhilarated, he regained the rock and rested. A thought occurred to him. If pike grew large and old tench could wax fat in the confines of the river, what gargantuan delights must fill *this* larder? The otter was earnest when he dived again.

Beyond the breakers, Lut fathomed the sea world stealthily. Rocks shelved to the bottom in ragged cliffs at whose feet a stony terrace spread to undulating sands, a drowned desert of florid oases and murky dunes. Kelp and sea cabbage grew there. Lush plantations swayed and shuddered. Who knew what skulked in their shadows? He hugged the rock.

As Lut descended a black head slid from a fissure and sniffed the seabed. It was the head of an eel, though no eel of the river, he thought with excitement, for the brute was enormous. This was an eel to do him justice. Keeping close to the cliff face, he peered down greedily.

'Come a little bit farther!' He watched the eel slither.

The dark head inched forward, lured by a sea worm. Lut hovered. 'A little farther. . . .' He waited.

With a sudden slide the eel left the rocks and was fully visible, longer than the otter, a thick muscular monster. Lut's eyes sparkled. In the diffused winter sunlight he noted features no common eel sported. The head was broad, the orb large. There were no scales. The eels Lut knew were scaly. Instead, the sea eel was clad in slime, a thick grease on which his gaping jaws clamped as the otter pounced. The

47

great conger, a female, showed her teeth. They were close-set and vicious.

'You'll pay! You'll rue your mistake!' Her eye was eloquent.

Lut felt the power of the monster, glimpsed the savage mouth, its fierce armament. Then, senses spinning, he was whirled in a circle and stood abruptly on his head. The eel was reversing, contracting backwards to her rock cave, tail seeking its entrance. Lut held on. The tail was lapping the crevice, prepared to lever him inside. The conger flexed. 'Come in, otter.' He saw the hole drawing nearer. 'Let us fight in the darkness!'

He kicked upwards. With a jerk he forced the monster's head with him, interrupting the retreat, and her tail lashed the rock face. It found a limpet-scabbed outcrop. Anchored, the eel took the strain.

Lut tugged frantically. The giant refused to budge. He heaved and paddled. If he could not land her quickly he had at least to haul her to the surface, for his breath was escaping, forced out by the struggle. Luck was kind. With a splurge, the knob of rock disintegrated and the conger, bereft of mooring, streamed up at his bidding. But only fleetingly. Next moment, the slimy coil enwrapped the otter and the eel's jaws were snapping. Lut bored at the neck. Like a terrier, he shook it. And now the eel twirled him crazily, convulsed by his mauling, yawing this way and that, madly spinning until the seabed and the marbled ceiling seemed to merge in Lut's awareness. He clung giddily. The conger scissored. Bucking, spiralling, she drove for deep water, Lut still attached to her.

Otter pride kept him fighting, a wild conceit. He could feel the eel's flowing fury, the power in the monster. Lut meant to land her. The voracious sea serpent had other plans. Through drowned gardens she flailed him, through swaying pollack-browsed forests and fields where wrasse lurked, where squid and cuttle fled jetting black fluid. Pebbles scattered, lashed by the tail of the conger. Shells rose, rocking back with quirky motions. Lut bit deeper. Very slowly the eel was tiring and he rode the brute upwards, the sea lightening in colour. His lungs were bellowing.

Hurling spume, the beasts surfaced. For a while they threshed the wave trough, then again the eel plunged, Lut borne down with her. But her charges were shortening. Now the otter, breath replenished, made his play for the seashore. The tiring serpent fought in bursts. The fight was gruelling. Time and again she raced downwards, Lut trailing, reserving strength for the eel's flagging spasms. Then the otter wrestled beachwards, abetted by the rollers. Enraged, the conger whipped and scythed. Purple-grey in the shallows, her greasy length smashed and pounded. Lut tugged wearily. Exhausted, he had almost beached his quarry when, with unexpected violence, she jerked and streaked for the breakers.

Lut jabbed four feet in the sand. Skidding, he strove to hold the fleeing monster. Dying wavelets creamed around them. The tug of war was long and stubborn. Both ways it lurched with slow and slithering uncertainty, eel and otter wasted. Now and then a more forceful wave doused them. Hissing foam washed their bodies. Then the conger was gasping. Somehow, Lut had hauled her dry and, biting deeply, found the nerve at her spine. Still the giant writhed and laboured. A final tailburst whipped the otter and her death throes were over. Lut did not move. He was shattered, scarcely conscious on the shingle.

Just how long he lay recovering he did not know. The margin of sand and pebble above the outgoing water grew broader as he rested, and shore birds, returning to forage, landed beside him. Once Caesar had remarked on the tides there, whose strength and neap variations produced great sweeps of sandy beach washed and nourished by the billows. Gulls squabbled. Oystercatchers searched the tideline. Trotting forward, they paused, red eyes beady, still as the rocks; trotting onwards after a moment. At sea, a mastlike neck bobbed until the cormorant upended. Time dissolved. Unaccounted by the rollers, by their ceaseless trip and founder, it eluded the otter. Clouds reassembled. They dimmed the sun. And as it gradually faded, something darkened the dunes where snow was visible.

Fingertaker nosed the margin.

Wiry fronds speared from the drifts which bore his tracks through the sandhills. Shuffling forward, he sniffed the litter of high water. The dry line was strewn with jetsam: lumps of wood, the tousled feathers of gulls along with withered sea holly and lifeless tangles of bindweed. The big otter's gaze wandered. Towering up, he smouldered. His angry watch spanned the shingle, falling fiercely on the conger. Nearby, the sand-daubed figure of Lut reclined exhaustedly. For a moment, the other paused – then, with a hiss of frustration, drew back in the grasses. The oystercatchers had flown. Far off, he heard voices.

'What's that?'

'Where?'

'By the water.'

The couple strode briskly, a young man and a girl, well wrapped against the weather. 'Too distant,' said the first. 'Could be some sort of creature. Could be a drowned dog.'

'Except it's moving.'

'You're right.'

'It's seen us. It's creeping into the sea. Oh, we'll miss it,' squealed the girl. 'Come on, you're such a *dawdler*. Do move yourself. . . .'

The boy, stumbling across the snowfield, was thankful to reach a lane where the fall had been compacted by tractor tyres. It was quiet, uncannily silent. He thought of the valley, its sheltered banks. In the hardest of frosts you heard life there: the ringing bark of the fox, the owl's hoot. At dusk the chinking of blackbirds and clamour of roosting pheasants were cheering company. The coldness carried their echoes. Here the white marsh was lifeless. No woods or coombes offered cover. For miles, flat eye-grinding snow glared up at a grizzled sky, lonesome and dazzling.

He squinted painfully. Shunning the vista, he dwelt on patches of darkness by dyke and roadside, small light-absorbing crannies which rested his eyesight. In these few snow-free nooks even now growth was stirring: heads of nettle, jagged dandelion clusters. Green mosses matted old clumps of withies. In snarles of crystal-roofed bramble, the brown of dead leaves gave relief from the whiteness. But the chill was inescapable and the boy, head lowered, winced as he followed the tyre tracks.

A pair of crows stood on the road, flying up as he approached. They had been pecking a carcass. It was a rabbit. Not long killed by some vehicle, the beast was intact and he plucked it from the snow. Lut liked rabbit. With his knife, the boy harled it, slitting one rear leg and threading the other through it to make a loop. By this he hung the animal from a twig in a clump of holly, too high for a fox, too prickly for the corvids. He shuffled on. It would be there when he returned.

Soon after, the sound of voices drew him forward. Two men were shovelling snow near a vehicle. It was stuck in a drift. For a moment he stood and watched, his jeans freezing. If he helped, they might guide him to a farm, even give him a lift. He was about to approach when the van became clearer, its snow-caked profile remembered. The boy saw the men straighten. 'Hey, you!' The first remover had glimpsed him. The fat one was glaring. 'That's him! That's the filching little joker!' They had thrown down their shovels.

The youngster was running. In the wilderness of his mind he saw the beasts piled in the wagon, the charnel house in the snowdrift, and did not wait to know his own fate. Leaping, he raced like a stag, scrambling back on his tracks, eyes boring the white haze. The cold road twisted. Beyond the point where he had joined it, the tracks doglegged and he saw clumps of scrubby growth. He slipped. Sprawling on his chest, he jumped up, his anorak an icy cuirass. Then the snowy bushes screened him and, boughs brushing his cheeks, he pushed on to a frosted garden, its cabbages mantled white, and found the cottage before him. Stealing around it, he crouched at its rear, breathing heavily.

'Well?'

He was listening for the men. The woman's query surprised him. 'Well, don't just stand there,' she prompted. 'What do you want? You've got a tongue.'

'I was seeking the way.'

'To where?' She hugged her arms fiercely, tight-lipped, hair ashen streaked with weasel shades of ginger. 'Way to *where*? And where have you come from?'

'I'm looking for provisions.'

'Out here!' The woman's snort was derisive. Less harshly,

she added, 'Good Lord, child, you're shaking,' and, brusquely solicitous, she wheeled him indoors. 'Lord's sake, look what you're wearing! Best come into the warm. I'm heating some soup; sit and wait for it.' The place was steamy, small and spotless. The boy's face glowed. Sliding to the window, he was peering out for the removers when her fist took his scruff and he was swung to the table. The woman smoothed a broad apron. 'Sit *still*, child,' she ordered. 'Keep the place tidy. Sit still and thaw out.'

He eyed the pot on the cooker. It was bright like the kitchen, all polished and shining. And safe from his pursuers. He considered its mistress. She moved briskly from stove to table and, though he flinched, the urchin felt well protected. 'There, it's hot. Take some bread and don't spill it.' She stood watching, arms akimbo. 'My, you're ravenous!' she said as he guzzled. 'I'm not surprised – on the marsh in this weather.'

'The marsh is all right.'

'All right?' She smiled grimly. 'Child, I was born here. I know what the marsh is. It can take you round in circles till you don't know north from south, nor what you came to discover. It puts a spell on you. Oh aye, it's romantic, soft enough when the sun shines and little churches pop their spires up; when the willow wands turn orange and sheep fill the grazings. What sheep, eh? Great plump wethers, a hundred pounds apiece and white as my bed sheets. But that's not the winter. In winter,' she said, refilling the soup bowl, 'just take care on the marsh for it can show you its claws, child, turn around on you in a minute.'

'Like a rat in a corner?'

'Something like,' she said, sniffing.

'Or an otter. I s'pose,' he probed. 'You got otters on the marsh? I mean, you'd know, being born there.'

'Otters is it! You're too late, child, for otters. Once,' she said, 'we named places for otters—Otter Dyke, Otter Crossing—and fell asleep to their whistling. Once, we'd creep to the pools and watch otter cubs playing. Now they've perished. Maybe there's two or three left: the big old dog, the wee bitch along the beech copse. Soon, *they'll* vanish. Otters! Doomed as dodos, destroyed by men, child. As men destroy all wild creatures, all God's blessing of beasts. There'll be a reckoning! When all we've left are our lice. Do you pray? Do you go to church Sundays?' She regarded him sternly. 'I doubt it. I doubt you've washed since the autumn.'

'The beech copse?'

'Bless my soul, boy, the heronry! Due east, in the beech tops. Where've you been? Not the marsh if you don't know the beeches!' She leaned closer, demanding, 'Let's hear where you came from. The truth, young man.'

He shrugged, no slouch at deception. That was part of surviving, the craft of the urchin's kingdom: of pike who lay loglike in ambush, fowl feigning injury, the sham indifference of the fox. 'Got stuck.' He eyed her, his mouth full. 'With some men in a van. I left them digging it out.'

'Came to look for provisions?' The woman's face had turned flinty. 'They sent you shopping on the *marsh*?'

'They're removers. We're moving.'

'Not from here; not until I know more.'

'I ought to be going.'

'There's cake,' she rasped. 'Have some cake.'

'Got to leave.'

'Without cake? A boy who doesn't want cake! Child, I've reared four myself; I know a lie when I hear one. Removers!'

'They'll be waiting. I'll slip out round the back.'

Strong arms pushed him down. 'Stay where you are.' She turned the door key and took it. Her gaze transfixed him, then she stepped to the passage. 'Don't you dare move, young man. I'll be back for you.' He heard a phone click.

Tiptoeing to the passage, the boy caught snatches of muffled chatter. He returned to the table. Slicing two chunks from the woman's cake, he stuffed them in his pockets, went quietly to the window and slipped the catch. Wriggling through, he tumbled back to the snow. For a second he paused, then made hotfoot for the gate. There was no sign of the removers. He scrambled quickly to the holly. Taking down the harled rabbit, he slung it on his shoulder. A hare's trace crossed his path, wide-spaced clusters of paw marks, free ranging. He went with them, veering back to the river.

As the snow thawed, the sluices gushed. While the marsh lay below high-tide level, most of the region was above the sea at low water so that, for maybe half a dozen hours in twenty-four, drainage was practical. By pipes and ditches, fluid streamed from the inned land, passed by dykes to larger channels then by river and sluice through the coastal wall. At such times the whole network of waters was on the move. Sedges swayed, tidegates rumbled. The pumps were churning as Lut returned to the foreshore and shook the sea from him.

For a while he had dossed on the rocks. Now, the man and girl gone, he came back for the conger, but the big eel had vanished. The otter bristled. Great webbed prints marked the sand. Unmistakably Fingertaker's, they led to the dunes, the drag marks of the conger along with them. Lut followed. His hard-won prize lay in a hollow. The head was eaten, the coils gritty and besmirched. He growled his fury. Circling, he chittered his outrage, snarling up at wheeling seabirds who mocked his misfortune. He swore at them. Thick with anger, he tracked inland where the scent of otter led him, his nose quivering.

Dusk darkened the marsh. Drooping sootily, it turned the reeds purple-brown. The hastening waters caught its shadows. By the cornices of banks, where moorhens skulked, snipe enjoyed a late supper. Their shrill calls reached Lut through the half-light: 'Fingertaker has passed! Beware the Lord of the Sedges, the hunter of hunters! The night is dangerous!' Small creatures, shrews and mice, climbed to safety as dykes brimmed, flooding their shelters. The rising waters alarmed the tunnellers.

On one tiny island, their velvet coats sodden, a mole and a pair of pigmy shrews shivered, afraid to brave the torrent. Lut passed without interest, his hunger dulled by choler. The otter's jaws champed for battle. Above, the air was stirred by swans homing, their wings creaking, pounding frosty twilight. They planed down to the river; and Lut, watching their landing, lost the trail of Fingertaker where it entered the current.

Lut took stock of his surroundings. He had regained the stream at its confluence with a disgorging flood channel, an old canal first created as a ditch against foreign invasion in Napoleon's time. Now, ranging far through the marshes, its function was drainage, banks bleak in the winter, tidegate open. Beside the lock stood a stone keeper's cottage and a red-painted lifebuoy, dim in the gloaming. Something moved. Eyes glinted, then the mink dissolved in darkness.

'Wait,' said Lut. 'Did the otter come this way?'

'He came this way.' The voice spat from the shadows. 'This is *his* gate. Pass at peril. Fingertaker is mighty.'

'Old,' snapped Lut. 'Fingertaker is *old*. The old one is doomed.'

'All otters are doomed.' The eyes were hostile.

Lut breasted the flurry. He said, 'Stay hidden, small cousin – my mood isn't gracious,' and, stroking between the sluice walls, issued to the smooth canal thinking: Hide, mink, for today I killed the conger and you, too, can be dealt with. But the glossy road beckoned, a black surface stretching out through dark shoulders to where stars were appearing, and the otter swam with purpose. The water whispered. On the banks, lonely sentries, pollards rose from lank growth in bizarrely twisted postures. Lut eyed them with suspicion.

The marsh had quietened, stiffened into its frost shell. Night deepened and now the trail returned strongly, scent thick in the sedges, admonishing caution.

Ears flat, Lut inched forward. He had moved to the reed band, chest-deep amid stems, turning quickly at their noises, snarling at shadows. Every hair on him tingled. His tail twitched with tension. 'Come and fight,' he murmured fiercely, then with growing apprehension, 'What keeps him? Come, and let's be done, old one. Let the night have a verdict.' But the darkness was empty. An east wind touched the channel. Cloud tongues licked the mounting Pleiades and, through strands of the rack, the shifting glow was uncanny. It made ghosts of lingering snowdrifts, cast false lights on the water. It played with Lut's nerves. Darting glances to his flanks, the animal advanced in impatient bursts.

A lapwing wailed; its sighing plaint filled the marsh dome. And now the cloud, snuffing stars, plunged flood and bank into blackness. Chill draughts eddied. They bore the trace of Fingertaker, the otter odour. Lut's lip curled. Teeth bared, he strained to catch a threatening movement, but heard only the water. Unmoving, he listened. The flow hummed and tittered. For a minute Lut could see little, then the cloud vapours lifted and the moon's crown topped the landline, flaring and brilliant. It lit the banks, silhouetting elm and willow. Looking up, Lut saw the beast's towering shade against the white orb.

Neck lofted, the great dog otter bestrode the night like some monolithic outcrop. The giant's challenge was daunting, an earth tremor. 'Stop. No farther.'

Lut trembled. 'I go where I want to.'

'You transgress in my kingdom.'

'You took my kill; is that not a transgression?'

'I am Lord of the Marshes.' Moonlight framed the king of battles. 'Look and quake, for Fingertaker confronts you! The conqueror!'

'The old one. You are *old*, Fingertaker.' Lut gulped. 'Don't think,' he dissembled, 'that your reputation scares me. Lut knows no frontiers. I've come for the female, the small sleek bitch of the marshes. I mean to take her home, old one. When I find her.' The notion emboldened him – he said with passion, 'I shall find her. I'll search the marsh until I find her.'

The black shadow did not move.

Water moaned. There was a long intermission before the answer crossed the hoarfrost. 'You must die.' It was a judgement. 'You must die like a ratling; you must snap like a marsh reed. For I am Lord of the Survivors and she belongs to me.'

'Lut, where are you? I've brought you a rabbit.' The boy cursed as the light failed. Ice still cluttered the current but the punt was free, tugging gamely at her painter. They could have been on their way, sailed long since, had Lut made an appearance. Instead, the lad had watched and waited, periodically calling. 'Don't let me down, Lutra. I'm back at the boat; come and join me.'

For a while he had been busy. Checking his gear, he had made the craft shipshape, clearing out mess and water. Now and then he had scanned the river, alert for ripples, but he had not seen the otter. Lut's absence distressed him. To kill time, the boy cut a crude mast and a yard from a sapling. The task was pointless. He was too cold to remove his jacket, the only possible sail. But it stopped him thinking of Lut in trouble, of Lut deserting his shipmate, of worse catastrophes.

'Heck, Lut, we're pals. You can't just push off at this stage!' But in his heart the boy knew the otter could, for he was wild and would do as the wild commanded. 'All right,' the plea was despairing, 'stay where you are, if you must. I'll come and look for you.'

The boy paused. For a time he quizzed the sedges then, unhitching the rotten painter, levered out from the mooring and shaped for deep water. The gloom was thickening. Chunks of ice rapped the hull and he steered by soggy islets, gaze probing, sweeping the mudbanks. Mallard sprang as he ghosted past. A streak of blue shot up river. He scarcely saw the kingfisher, being so intent on blobs in the water, knobby shapes which might have been a head bobbing, but turned out to be shadows. 'Lut, I'm coming downstream. If you're there, wait and join me.' A black tree stump raised hopes, then a weed-skirted boulder. Deceits were rife in reeds and thickets.

Endless sallows loomed damply. He baled water. His repairs had been sketchy and the hull boards seeped where the caulking was absorbent. Encroaching night dimmed his hopes. Soon the confluence faced him. It presented a dilemma. Ahead, on the main stream, he could see anchored vessels. He thought Lut would have shunned them. The canal was deserted, touched by starlight, a more probable bearing. Yet the tidelock was daunting, its overflow a torrent. He consulted his compass. It was no larger than a penny, a pocket toy, but the needle twitched and he let it stop swinging. The channel led east. Convinced, the boy steered for the open gates.

It was dark there. A window glimmered in the cottage; a washing line fluttered. He thought the shadows would conceal him. More frightening than discovery, the swirling race bid to thwart him and, leaning to the pole, he heaved with all his strength. The craft jibbed. He fought the water. The lock's bottom was smooth. Precariously, he purchased on flanges, small projections in the walls, inching forward. A slip could be disastrous. If he went over, the punt would shoot backwards, boy and boat swirl apart down the river. He felt dizzy. Lurching, he almost plunged to the current. Somehow, clutching the inner gate, he kept his balance, gained the channel and hauled the punt to slack water.

He had lost the pole but still had oars and a paddle, and the dark cut was tranquil. Resting a moment, he pulled away from the lock cottage. 'Lut?' he called softly. 'Did you come this way, Lutra?' The moon was rising. It fingered parts of the channel, making stripes through the pollards. 'Lut?' The boy heard a faint scuffling. He raised the paddle. The punt whispered, sliding gently. The commotion was distant but now distinct, water splashing, reeds rustling. He eased the blade into the flow, drew it back. The old boat purred. He heard a squeal and sounds of threshing in the sedges. Shipping the paddle, the boy crawled to the foredeck, lying prone like a fowler. The reeds rhumba-ed.

With sudden violence, a shape burst to the bank, hissing viciously. Jaws agape, the otter rounded. The boy watched in astonishment. He had never seen Lut so fearsome. The beast was ugly, coat in spikes, mouth distorted. The sound he made was obscene, an explosion of hatred. Then, madly as the first, a second otter erupted, crashed from the sedges. The boy gasped. The brute was monstrous. It made Lut look puny. Rampant, the otters closed, wet coats streaming, water spraying as they battled. In seconds the bank was drenched, then ferociously they rolled to the reedbed, a snarling tangle, clawing and mauling as stems flattened around them. The margin frothed.

Now mud draped them, made masks of faces as contorted as the gargoyles in Hunter's Hall. Now the reeds were in turmoil. The beasts were gone. Now the mid-flow was boiling as they rose there. Teeth flashing, they towered from the channel, the monster's fangs at Lut's neck.

'Lut!' The boy grabbed an oar. 'Flaming heck, Lut, he'll kill you!' Bawling, he hammered the water. 'Get away from each other!'

Still the dog otters fought. They were obsessed, deaf and blind to intrusion. 'Stop!' the boy bellowed wildly. His platform wobbled. At last, punting towards them, he saw them freeze, their eyes swerving. The larger beast met his gaze. There was murder in its visage, then it sped away, diving. Lut sank torpidly. 'Lut? Are you hurt?' The urchin crouched at the gunwale. His relief was uncertain. 'Come on up. Are you wounded?'

The otter surfaced to starboard. Lut shook himself in the water. Droplets shimmered. Dunking, he shook again, growling after Fingertaker. For a while he swam boastfully then, slithering inboard, took post in his corner. He licked his guard hairs. The otter's manner was smug – too smug, the boy reckoned. He said, 'You're lucky I came. If I hadn't come looking. . . .' He drove the punt up the water. 'If I hadn't come searching, the brute would have killed you. So much for not waiting! You might have been patient. I wasn't long.'

They sailed east through the moonlight. Clouds were scudding, the wind sudden as it rose on the marshes. The boy pulled up his collar. 'Tell you what, though, I was right: we're going to find you a mate, Lut, somewhere ahead.

When the day comes. When we can scout for the beech crowns.' The wind was roughing the surface. The otter ignored it. Neither the boy nor the wind mattered; he had survived Fingertaker, proved his worth against the old one. Lut smirked. He had fought like an athlete, swerving, stabbing with brilliance. He had confounded the monster, refused to die.

He growled, reliving the battle: the giant against the poacher. The poacher prince! Nimble-witted and agile! The war was not over. Next time he would dazzle, make rings round the marsh lord. Lut was pitched from his reverie. There was a crunch and the punt foundered. Something sharp and submerged had pierced the hull. It tore like paper. Boards flew upwards. In their place, he saw the hole. And half the canal seemed to pour through it.

The outboard whined. Cutting the engine, the boatman put in obliquely to the riverbank. The tide was making, filling creeks and small inlets. It crept and oozed around reed stems, insinuated into hollows, crawled and swirled into mud pans. The boatman thought of the boy and of the cold, relentless water. Hunter stood forward. The chill cut through him, stabbed them both. His cowled eyes shifted. 'Take her in by that spit. I want to look at the hummock. The *spit*, man, you'll miss it!'

'I'll take her in, mister. Don't tell me where to put her.'

'Damned Bolshie!'

The boatman swung the helm, glowering. 'Blamed dictator!' He pulled the peak of his cap lower. 'You old despot.' There was madness in Hunter, but who else could follow the otter – find the trail – like the tyrant? Who but Hunter knew the signs: a few faint paths, a place where something had rolled, prints which to the boatman seldom looked twice alike? Three toes, four toes – the seals varied with the mud. Where it was soft, all five digits were scored, the trace of webbing sometimes evident. More often the tracks were

61

blurred. But Hunter knew them. Hunter knew the otter's tail mark, and where Lut had eaten.

Now the mound drew the tracker, for otters used such sites for sprainting. Hunter knew where spraint was likely. 'Heave to!' he had bawled, and they had searched beneath bridges. They had found spraint on ledges, boulders, where streams joined the river. Once, the man had waved glumly, calling 'Mink!' and they surged on. Otter spraint had a sweet smell. Hunter knew it from that of mink, and its age by its colour: grey when old, dark when fresh. The spraint which marked the mound was dark, flecked with fish scales. A small disc, the undigested lens of a roach's eye, lay in it.

The nine-fingered man straightened. 'We're getting close. The trail's holding to the river.'

He winced, arthritic as the hound which had scrambled from the boat. They were both old, thought Hunter with anger. The winds got into them. Like old trout, long past spawning, they lost more to the winters than the summers had to give them. It came to all things. Eventually the trout's eyes grew sightless, its head large as its body wasted, fins unequal to the current. Then the fish sought the weeds. There, in ultimate seclusion, its gills heaved and it keeled over. Hunter gritted. His gills were not finished, his bones not yet for the crayfish. He cursed the winter. He damned the wind and the marshes.

'Hunter?' The boatman's voice was carried sideways.

Hunter watched the dog wading. He saw once more the hounds in the water, their flanks gleaming, breath rising. He could still hear the clamour. It haunted him. In his mind he saw the otter, limp, quiescent near the bottom. The great dog otter. Hounds were whimpering. Hunter's hand had plunged deeply. The stream was cool, tingling on wrist and forearm. He had reached down, stretched far down to the beast he took for lifeless. Then had leaped upwards, howling, a mangled stump for a finger. He remembered the pain, the sight of blood spurting. Pain and bloodshed. . . .

And Fingertaker had gone.

The easterly gusted.

'You all right?' roared the boatman.

'All right?' The wind seared. 'Of course, you fool. Get the

damned engine started. I say he's still on the river. Get aboard.' Hunter straddled the gunwale. He snarled, heaving the dog in, 'Get the damned machine revving. Full speed, fellow. Once it's dark we'll be stymied.'

The prow rose and their wake washed the sedges. The air was bitter. Gusts of sleet swept the marsh, disturbing wildfowl. Redshanks rose in restless flocks. The first geese of the evening lifted, beating inland. There were a dozen in the skein, voices clangorous. Hunter scowled. They were no more than a gunshot high, a 'right and left' had he been fowling. Now their ringing notes mocked him. The boatman watched them. '*Aang-aang*' – skein on skein of geese were coming, yawing above the whins on the dunes. Greys and pink-legs. Duck flew everywhere. Then they had passed and a single bird, the owl-like harrier, hung over the polder as dusk approached.

The chill had deepened. The helmsman thought about the urchin. A slim shape with rod and line; a lad on a jetty. What did they know of him? He came and went – and told lies. It was not much. And could have floated to disaster. Reeds were moaning. The marsh's music was eerie, a soulful drone through which geese cried and cackled. The outboard's yap broke their chanting. Its wave slapped and clouds flitted.

'There!' Hunter gestured towards the willows. 'Take her in by the scrub.' Ashore once more, they climbed the bank to the moorhen. The fowl was dead in the grasses, legs twisted. Long and spurred, such legs could rip a man's flesh or slay a rival in the spring. Their power had not saved the creature. Its breast was eaten. 'Our friend!' Hunter turned, his face flushed. 'We're on his heels, the webbed beggar.'

'Or a fox. What makes you think it was the otter?'

'The bird's intact. Just the tender meat's eaten. That's an otter.'

'And a fox?'

'A fox pulls his prey to pieces.' Hunter snarled his impatience. A fox left little for the crows. The men stood hunched in the squall, icy rain in their faces. The boatman cursed. It was late. Hunter knew about otters – but he could not hold off the night. They would be beaten by the darkness.

'Are we much behind, mister?'

'Two, three hours. The kill's recent.'

'The night's beat us.'

'We need lights. Could still hunt if we had lights.' Hunter brightened. 'By God, the lock cottage, damn it. . . .' They went on, the boat's exhaust a blue pennon. The engine echoed. It was about six o'clock when the lock keeper, responding to their shouting, produced rescue lamps and joined them. Within an hour they had found Lut's tracks by the channel and were heading east.

The boy was swimming. As the punt hit the obstruction he had pitched forward, deluged as she opened. The wreck filled instantly. Next moment he was striking for the bank, breath snatched by the freezing water. His clothes dragged, and in sudden, choking panic he threshed like a mad creature until, feet touching the bottom, he lurched to the sedges. Gasping, he sprawled by the channel, mud wrapping him.

Thin bare trees lined the cutting. Amid their shadows he glimpsed oars floating and a square prow, grotesquely tilted. It settled lower, the rest already below the surface, and the boy saw the otter slowly circumnavigate the wreckage, then haul from the water and climb the bank. In the trees, the beast paused. Unconcernedly, Lut scratched. The boy was shaking. Drenched, he struggled up calling, 'Lut, hang about,' but the otter had gone.

The boy trailed him up the floodbank. At the top the wind was savage. Clouds careered in the night sky, hurling spite at the marshes, creating wild zones of darkness from which the moonlight fled, wraithlike. It roamed the flats with freakish humour. Dykes met where it shimmered, bleak vistas of polder unrelieved by habitation. The boy saw neither roof nor cable. He looked back at the channel. His hopes had sunk there. The old punt had been their mainstay; now her journey was ended, his own a nightmare of survival. His teeth rattled.

The flats were spooky. Smugglers' tales told of marsh ghosts – methane seeping from the turf, the boatman had reckoned, but the lad was uncertain. The place encouraged phantasms. A drawn-out cry rent the evening. It was beyond the boy's explaining, almost human in its anguish, long and

64

yammering, increasing his fear. As it died he saw Lut scout-·
ing forward. The beast dropped into a ditch. Dripping
sludge, the urchin followed, crouching low in the rushes.

'Hang about' – the wind was howling above him – 'I can't
keep up with you, Lut!'

Body bent, the boy fared blindly down the dyke. His feet
squelched; he ran with one higher than the other, holding
close to the swill so the banks afforded cover, sometimes
hemmed by brittle sedges. The effort warmed but exhausted
him. When he paused, the cold tormented. From time to
time he heard the otter, or saw its sleek body shining. Once,
the creature left cover, exploring a sheep track. The path,
raked by knifing zephyrs, led the boy across innings and over
several small bridges. Deprived of shelter, he trembled.

Something passed his head, screaming. Sound and
movement merged weirdly, veering off then returning,
changing tone as the disturbed plover wheeled. The screech
was doleful but less so than the throbbing; the sob of wings in
the darkness. The sound died and another dyke beckoned.
This time the boy barely made it, tumbling feebly down the
incline to lie near the bottom. The punt was two miles
behind him. Not a light had he spotted – two miles of marsh
and not a farmstead. At length his steps had grown weaker
until he just wished to stop there. The cold would numb and
overwhelm him. The pain, he thought, would be short-lived.
Peace would follow.

But he got to his feet. Lut was somewhere ahead and he
groped onwards. Reeds engulfed him. Their dead seedheads
flicked his cheeks, unseen fingers in the wind. The sky was
murky. Then the racing clouds split apart and the moon lit
the marshscape. 'Lut?' A ewe bolted. Boy and sheep alike
were startled and, in the glare, the lad could see puddled
grass as far as the stars, a silvered mat on which moats coiled
like serpents. His gaze searched the bleak grazing. 'There's
something there, Lut – a shelter.'

The structure was vague, like a mirage on the levels. No
lane served it. It stood afar, isolated, without tree or bush for
friendship. The walls were low, the roof high. It might have
been a small haybarn, or more aptly, it struck the youngster,
an ark on the floodland. The path was circuitous. Broad

65

pools lay in the grazing, and twisting dykes forced diversions. Great shaggy sheep loomed from hollows, their wool combed by the easterly. At last, where a plank traversed a ditch, he reached a plain wood-framed window and, peering in, saw the font. Sheep dung littered the ground. Hugging the wall, the boy crept through the wind to the lonely door.

Sedges droned. He met no tombstones or memorials, just bare earth where the marsh sheep of centuries had sought the lee. Inside, the floor was brick, wood-pinned timbers mounting into the roof with bluff simplicity. The boy paused. Moonlight streamed in the doorway. There were eight pews, each with its own gate and latch. Like lamb pens. In the silence the urchin slumped on a bench, barely conscious of the surroundings. A little altar stood near him, and in the gloom he saw an eye. The wind was blessedly absent. His pew was dry. The eye held him. It was wide, inscribed in gold on aged boarding – the eye, he thought, of the owl, of a fox in the night. The eye of leveret and badger – of the deer in the van. *I AM* proclaimed the legend.

The urchin started in confusion. The door was creaking. He tracked it back into focus by his own muddy footprints. It had swung in the draught, now half open, a slab of light where smocked shepherds once entered – and the otter was snuffling. 'Lut?' The beast froze. Drawing back, Lut stood listening. The boy's voice was a croak.

'Lut, you've got to keep marching, bearing east. You've got to look for the beech tops, take the line of the herons. For where they nest, the bitch lodges.' The words came faintly. 'Listen, Lut. . . .'

Lut gleamed in the starshine.

'You must make her your mate, Lut. Take her back to the vale, stock the river, fill the holts with young otters. You can find her. You can make it alone now . . . so don't wait . . . I'm not coming. Just march, you scrounging brown demon!'

Lut heard no more. Shifting position, he saw the crumpled form, now on the floor, and assumed the boy was sleeping.

The otter quit the doorway. Sheep were huddled by the wall. For a while he prowled around the building. In daytime, snipe and swans fed there but now the ewes were alone, and Lut dossed in the sedges. Until the small hours he catnapped then slipped into the water. Lamps were shining. Tuned to danger, he watched the men approaching.

A dog was leading them. They had disembarked near the wreck, the old hound's interest quickening as the trail crossed the innings. The men had followed. Cussing and slithering, lamps stabbing, they had probed the long reedy drains and, traversing Five Watering Sewer and Highknock Channel, come at last to the grazings. Lut heard their voices. 'The church!' Hunter was urging as the otter dived.

Part Two

The Marsh Bitch

Clouds passed in dreary rabbles, wind brusque in the treetops. It tugged the hair of the woman on the jetty and she pulled on a headscarf. Spring was still some weeks distant yet the woman, driving out in the car, had seen coltsfoot flowering, and primrose. At one spot, she had seen aconites blooming. It might be winter in the town but out here birds were courting and the first lambs had suckled.

She said, 'It's quiet here. Where I work it's all traffic.'

The boatman grunted. He had just driven the rats off, hurling stones at them. Up the bank, the water vole, hearing their snuffling, had fled from his tunnel to the stream, where he stopped suddenly. Peering into the depths, the podgy vole had seen the sludge-coloured shadow and, undeceived by its stillness, pulled back in terror. The pike looked lifeless but his barbed trap was lethal. The vole trembled. Appalled, he had scampered to a tree stump, a hollow pollard, scrambling into it. There he crouched, eyes popping, cheeks puffed with fright.

'Quiet and peaceful,' said the woman.

The boatman climbed from the wherry.

'You crossing?' he asked her.

'No.' She gazed at the river. 'I've just been to the Hall. It's so lovely around here, so much stirring: herb-Robert, chervil, wild parsley. In town it's either summer or winter. In the country the seasons merge with each other. I saw a bee in the lane. It hardly seems. . . .'

'You've seen Hunter?' the man said.

'About the boy.' She smiled, her face harassed, younger than it looked, broad and sensible like her plain leather shoes. The man approved of them. 'Welfare,' said the woman. 'I'm from the Child Care Department.' Then, 'Why, look, there's a heron! It's time he left for the heronry.'

'Aye.' The man quizzed her darkly.

He viewed the heron. Harn was fishing. The fry swam at his feet. Early hatchers brought down on the current, they fed in shallow inlets, all fins and eyes. As Harn watched, they gleamed and darkened, sometimes almost transparent then dull as mud in the angled light. The boatman growled. 'Aye, old Harn there will leave us soon. How's the lad?' he asked gravely. 'Is there any improvement?'

'He'll be all right.'

'Luck o' the innocent. You or me, we'd have drowned or died of exposure. He looked bad when we found him.'

The man's gaze held the heron. The bird was motionless, observing the fry. It took practice to spot them. Harn was practised. He knew the fry of the loach from those of the trout – the first hugging the bottom, the second rising – and both kinds from the minnow, small in adulthood. He watched a stickleback. The horny dwarf could swim backwards. Harn knew where to find him, and the young of the pike, a precocious thug.

'A water scamp,' said the boatman.

The woman turned, eyebrows lifted.

'The lad – a water urchin.'

'Full of fibs,' she said frowning. She opened her handbag. 'I want to ask you about him. The child is less than forthcoming. Half the time you can't trust him. We need information and I thought you might. . . .'

'Has Hunter . . . ?' The boatman scowled at her notebook. 'That beggar knows nothing.' He looked away, conscience pricking. Without Hunter the lad most likely would have perished, sprawled unconscious in the marsh church, cold and sodden. But that was all. There it ended for Hunter; he had no time for the urchin. The boatman missed the youngster. 'Hunter knows less than I do, and that's not worth telling. Don't you listen to Hunter. Him nor I, we know nothing. Save,' the boatman said slowly, 'the lad's never a bad 'un. Don't be told he's a bad 'un. Wild and artful, but. . . .'

'I'm sure.' Rooks erupted from the oak crowns, tumbling down to the ploughland. 'I doubt,' the woman reflected, 'he's ever done a term's schooling or known a snug fireside.'

'He likes the water.'

'I can see the attraction.' She watched the current. 'Maybe he'll miss it at first, but then boys can't go drowning or facing life without schooling. He needs caring for,' she said with conviction. 'There'd be outings. That's if we took him into care.'

The boatman spat.

'We'd look after the child.'

'I don't say you wouldn't.'

'Well,' she said, 'we'll see, shan't we. . . .'

Harn heard but ignored them, a journey before him. First he dusted his beak and then scraped off the eel slime; he rinsed and shook the long dagger. The small fish had fled to crannies. He stretched his wings. Legs dangling, Harn went up towards the cloud bank, great sails tilting so the ground spun below him. The woods turned slowly, the man and woman grew smaller. Soon he saw other herons, mere dots, easting rhythmically. He called and they came closer. More birds were converging with steady beat.

The herons winged with sure purpose. Lut considered them glumly. Around him ranged dykes and polder, meres and mudflats, marsh hamlets. The scene bewildered him. Shingle deserts stretched seaward to fade in spume. Behind, lost in memories, the old shore stood deserted. Here, like lurchers, Viking longships had hunted; marshmen braced themselves for the onslaught of foreign fleets. Once, smugglers had toiled here, bearing brandy, tea, tobacco inland to Brenzett and Botolph's Bridge.

Unlike the birds, Lut was daunted. The bitch was small, the marsh massive. He searched sluices and tidegates but the dykes seemed unending, his quest overwhelming. He paused, flopping wearily. A beetle passed. Bronzed and glistening, it pursued its own odyssey, slogging on. Grey wings crossed the marsh platform. Lut caught a faint rustle. A weasel was foraging, pointed head darting. He watched the brisk creature. It was a flame – a flame that churred as it rippled. 'Follow the herons.' The white-bibbed dwarf eyed him fiercely. 'You don't belong here,' it whispered.

Lut growled, but he pondered. Where herons fished, so might an otter. The birds streamed over. As one vanished, another grew and dwindled. 'Aak!' they called as they travelled. The otter rose, his snout jutting. Plunging back to the reedbeds, he followed. Raking labyrinths enclosed him. He cleaved by dripping channels. Through the day he cruised the cuttings; by night, held his bearing. Diving, Lut swirled through sedges. Collies yapped and snipe scattered. Ewes, drinking, backed up in surprise as the otter passed.

At last he rested. Ahead lay a village. He let dusk fall then pressed on, nose working. An owl had perched on a gatepost. It flew off down an alley and Lut chanced the passage. It was quiet, deep in shadow. Halfway down, something shifted. It ghosted closer, became a soft-striding cat, claws unsheathed, her tail bristling. Lips drawn back, the cat spat through her eyeteeth. Lut drew breath.

'Psshtt!' He huffed with such violence the other fled.

The path emerged on a road.

A shaft of light struck the curb, a car parked beyond it. Lut growled. There was a strong smell of danger, and for some time he wavered. Close to the wall, he crept forward. The light splashed from a door, along with oily fumes of frying and harsh twangy voices, doubly loud in the stillness. Beyond, the road turned to gloom, dykes and sedges, but the bright rays were garish and Lut held back from them. A truck swung up the street. Shadows leaped and rotated. Then the demon charged on and Lut, shaking, saw a child step from the doorway. He ran forward. The boyish figure reassured him. As it turned away along the sidewalk, with its bag of chipped potatoes, Lut remembered the marsh church, the storm and snowdrifts, and how the boy had once saved him.

He had taken it for granted, undervalued the friendship. Now he craved nothing more. The lad scuffed his feet. A few steps and he turned. At first the otter simply stared, then began to growl quietly. The youth's face was unfamiliar. Lut was gazing at a stranger who gawped back, his mouth gaping. 'Wao-oo!' the boy yelled. His whoop brought others from the chip shop. Their voices blared. 'Seen a *what*, Jim? It was old Ned's dog, bet'cha!'

'What was?'

'What Jim seen.'

'It were duck-toed.'

'Geroff!'

Lut crouched in the shadows. He was under the parked car, flesh crawling. The street rang with their banter. Youths were scuffling and munching, dropping chips on the pavement. Someone stooped to tie a shoelace. 'By the heck,' the lad blurted, 'it's here, beneath the motor! That's never Ned's terrier. I never seen a dog *that* weird! Come and look at the creature. . . .' Lut did not tarry. Taking flight, the otter shot from his refuge, speeding like an arrow through the village on the crown of the road, across a junction of lanes and away from the dwellings.

'You should have seen him!'

'No kidding!'

The lane darkened. Before long there was water. Lut was back among the dykes and, swimming east for some minutes, reared up to glance behind him. A dim glow came from the buildings and he heard muffled shouting. He was safe in the channel. Relaxed, he paddled forward. Amber mink orbs were watching and moles breasted dykebanks. Their pink hands scrabbled. Scents of herb and turf mingled. The marsh grew wild as he travelled. Head back, the otter hurled his shrill whistle ahead of him.

Alone, he dozed in the rushes. Mallard swam near the hideout, plumply tempting but wary. Gulls sailed on air freshets. He had found food by the dyke: drowsy natterjacks and newts, some small fish. Now he napped with restless movements. For once Lut felt lonely. He missed the punt, the boy's voice. *'You've got to look for the beech tops, take the line of the herons. For where they nest, the bitch lodges. . . . You can find her. You can make it.'*

The otter stirred. The marsh was dangerous and his next test came quickly. A van had stopped on the polder. An old fox slipped beside him, neither owning the other, each watching the gunmen. Lut had barely awakened. It had a nightmarish quality. The fox broke from cover. There was a stunning explosion. The removers were firing and Lut could see mallard falling. He glimpsed their specula flashing. The fox had dropped, two legs shattered. It was attempting to crawl, hind limbs dragging, when Lut hit the water.

Still dazed, he heard the bellow. 'Leave the fox – there's an otter!'

'Where?'

'The dyke. Take the bank!'

76

Lut lay on the bottom. There was a bare foot of water and the men were above him, one behind, one ahead. Beyond the fat man, a pipe joined the cutting but the guns had it covered. A rough-stemmed weed, the stringy chara, hid the otter. He knew a twitch could betray him, and held his breath.

'Your end,' bawled the fat man. 'Drive him this way, I'll nail him.'

The sound drubbed in the water. Lut could see a gross belly. He scanned the channel. Soon, plantlife would splurge there: marsh woundwort and crowfoot. Until then the stretch was barren, caddis dotting the bottom, nymphs and larvae above them. The man's image threatened. A small willow cast shade and Lut flexed into its shadow. The removers were peering. All they saw was a shimmer; that and skittering pond gnats. Lut wriggled. The silt would swirl if he touched it, and he moved with his legs raised.

Air surfaced. Bubbles rose and the smaller man, whirling, lashed the water with gunshot. He cursed. The breath had gushed from a mussel. 'Rot the foot-mucking bilge, I can't see him!'

'He's not there.'

'Where?'

'Shift up. Keep your eye on the drain, it's the brute's only funk hole.'

Lut was almost beneath them. Making use of their distraction, he reached the bank near the fat man, slipping under its shoulder. A water scorpion fled him; ram's-horn snails pulled their heads in. For a while he was hidden but the pipe was still distant, scant cover intervening. A shock of willow moss beckoned. Lut dashed for the refuge with all his speed.

'There he goes – into the weed!'

'Hold fire, don't stir the mud. You could miss him in that lot. Let him show us his nose. . . .'

The otter lay still, eyes fearful. There was no course but to sprint for the tunnel, exposed to their gunfire. He had to get there. He could not fail at this stage, leaving the bitch to Fingertaker. He would not fall to the removers. Lut nerved himself for the effort. There were twelve yards, perhaps, to safety and he covered them jinking, swerving as he torpedoed, shot spraying the surface. It kicked silt from the bottom.

Four reports rocked the channel yet so quick was the otter, so elusive the image, that he reached the pipe unscathed, pushing deep into darkness. Lut lay panting in the tunnel. Air flowed with the water and he snarled as he gulped it. Satisfaction stole on him. He had foiled them; they could not match his talent. But he emerged with fresh caution. The van had gone and he found the fox hidden. It was dead, mask contorted by torment.

He was a prince of escapists – but he missed the punt.

The van roared through the evening. 'I'll have him,' said the fat man. 'The next time, I'll have him.' The driver jeered, his lip curling. He watched the lake gleam and darken. The headlights swung inland.

'We've a load. Forget the otter.'

'Till the next time.'

'Next time's planned. Hunter's deer herd.'

'Since when?'

'Since now, fat man. Since I made the decision. Some heavy humping won't harm you; you can sweat off the lard.'

The marsh lake fell behind. Fingertaker rose from it. His grizzled jaws quivered and, in the murk, his teeth glinted. He saw the van's rear lamps vanish, then ranged the shore, bristling. His rocking tread was unhurried. Birds and mammals feared his footsteps but Fingertaker was not hunting. Lut would come, and he waited. Nostrils flared, he smelled the night. Claws curved, he slashed divots. The great mere trembled darkly. Lut would snap like a marsh reed. The blow would fall.

Lut paused, dazzled. The lake, at sunrise, was pearly. He watched the herons fly over. They were not far from home now, some fishing the shallows. Soon the reeds became golden, plumed by fine wands of willow, and Lut approached slowly. Insects swarmed. Misty bays and creeks glittered. He saw the first stars of celandine flowering as he advanced.

Across the flats came the redshanks. Voices fluting, they

78

topped the rushes, rumps flashing. Then oystercatchers swept over. Briskly, they thrust past slower squadrons, pitching down to the mere's edge. The marsh was vibrant with birdlife. Lut saw snipe and crisp formations of dunlin. Gulls smothered small islands. Fork-tailed terns rode the zephyrs.

He ran down to the margin. Fleets of fowl sailed the waters. The lagoon was a magnet. Beamy coots pottered inshore. Duck and geese cruised the sounds: Brent and mallard, greys and widgeon. Swans swam languidly. Above all, winged Harn's kindred. He could hear their hoarse barking. Across the lake they were turning, the grey dots descending. Lut dunked. He could almost feel the welcome, the warmth of the greeting, as he shaped for the far shore with eager strokes.

'Aak!'

The great birds swept over.

Lut surged. Like a dolphin he gambolled and gulls scattered. Duck sprang, bellies sparkling. 'Stop me *now*, Fingertaker!' He skimmed, broad back curving. 'Stop me taking a marsh mate!'

'Aak! The herons are home!'

He climbed from the water.

Atop the bank he peered forward. It was hazy. He sniffed impatiently, unable to see much. A swampy patch filled the foreground, the rest lost in greyness, shading white towards the sky wall. The otter rose on his haunches. He saw only the herons, high over the vapour, the rest thickly misted. Then, abruptly, the sun warmed and the air cleared. Tracks appeared amid grasses, tufts gained definition. Lut watched the mist lifting. From its strands towered the heronry: the green mound, timber columns and lofted crowns.

Mauve and gold, the trees loomed like a castle, marsh citadel. Lut advanced. The mound grew slowly, often hidden by sedges, laggard mists. He ploughed the quagmire. Hot and muddied, he laboured. Great nests were in view now, like rafts in the treetops; huge trunks, white with birdlime. He stopped at last, by the old island.

Around the mound ran a gully, a small brook there. Grass bulwarks climbed smoothly. Here the herons were landing, marking time in strange obeisance. Lut looked on with awed interest. Heads tucked in, they stood in dozens, each broodingly silent. They seemed entranced, in homage to the marsh. Not one flicked a feather, nor did neighbours heed each other. The otter edged closer. A weird force had possessed them. Some, he saw, were changing colour, bills and feet turning red, or suffused with pink and orange. The colour deepened then faded.

More herons were descending. 'To the field,' their wings whistled.

'To the hallowed field of silence.'

They wheeled solemnly. As each came zigzagging down, the grey ranks briefly shimmied. Theirs was an odd, dreamy dance, wings half open, feet dragging, a kind of drowsy shuffle soon replaced by repose. Lut growled quietly. Abstrusely it continued, the blushing rite of the dance-gathering, birds arriving and leaving to seek their nests. In the trees they fell to neck-contorting courtship on the high rafts.

Lut lost patience.

He called, unanswered. The brook was silent. All it held were the reflections of herons and he felt himself cheated. He looked up fretfully. Above, he saw Harn, the old heron's crest flaunted, his gaze content. He had a young henbird with him. The otter snarled. He had not crossed the marsh to watch Harn take a partner. 'It's me – Lut!' There was envy in his anger. He snarled, eyes glaring. 'Where is she, Harn? I must know where to find her.'

But the beeches were tall. Harn did not respond.

The sky hurled ice. Hailstones drubbed the bitch otter. They bent the rushes which roofed her, and bounced on the marsh tracks. Everywhere missiles rattled, strewing ridges, filling furrows until the sun first congealed then dissolved them. In the brook they had made circles. She had pondered the ripples – larger than rain hoops, smaller than fish rings. One hoop had held her interest. It had grown, swirled strangely and vanished. Inquisitively, the bitch had dived.

Hail was melting. She moved with caution. The brook was narrow, little more than a gutter, bounded by bent grass and tangled reeds. Threading a loop, she saw the creature ahead, now breast-deep and ambling. Lut searched dismally. Creeping nearer, she watched him. She was shaking. Her soft roan coat tingled and her snub nose was twitching. The male turned, alerted. He had sensed being followed. Fangs bared, he swung on her then, amazed, squealed his pleasure. She waited.

Ecstatic, he joined her. As he did so, she cuffed him and they sparred in the shallows, standing upright like boxers so their loose-fitting pelts made folds at their midriffs. Water flew as they wrestled. Toppling, they rolled hugging in the gutter until Lut, hugely gleeful, bounced back and forth froglike while the playful bitch chased him. Growling, she grabbed his neck, tugging, worrying. Then, inviting him to follow, flew madly around the beech copse, snapping as he harried.

For a long time they mudlarked. At last, exhausted, they lay and dried in the sunshine. The female grew solemn. 'You shouldn't be here,' her glance said.

'Nor should you.'

'Fingertaker will find you.'

'We'll go to the river.' But, for now, they went nowhere, too weary for movement. Instead, they slept in the sedges until the shadows grew cooler, when Lut awoke with a start. This time the bitch was still with him. He relaxed. In a while she stretched, yawning, and he joined her with fervour. The evening was special. Not since cubhood had he hunted with another, and now he set out with her as an eager companion.

A clear sky glistened. The wind had veered to southwest, blowing warm through the rushes, a fragrance of spring in the grass and soil. As the two otters lolloped, the moon came up behind the heronry, large and yellow. They followed the brook, their progress leisurely. Softly paddling, they beached now and again to explore the banks. Slugs were stirring. They took a few – not the large, distasteful black ones but smaller kinds, which they relished.

A rabbit bolted.

Lut had roused it from a thicket and, as it scampered, they gave chase. The scut bobbed in the marsh grass. They trailed it. Nose to earth, the otters ran like giant ferrets, scent strong in their muzzles, brought at last to a dyke drilled with burrows. Lut watched the bitch disappear. He was too broad for the tunnels, but she was gone with a wriggle and he settled to wait. The holes were black. He grew uneasy. She could be stuck in the bury. Snout to earth, Lut sniffed anxiously.

For a while he was patient, then pawed the entrance. He was digging when at length she appeared from another hole. First, an earthy nose surfaced, then her tightly gloved hands. She shook briskly. 'Come on,' she called, 'let's go fishing!'

'No rabbit?'

She flounced off, undefeated. Who cared about rabbit? She knew a pool where the brook brimmed and soon they stopped by it. Little owls mewed like tomcats. The moon glared. With a bound the small bitch dealt the water a mighty splash.

Lut found the feast waiting. Her crude dive had caused panic, driving the fish to the edges where they sought shelter in holes and crannies. Some, with ostrichlike delusion, had poked their heads into nooks, bodies visible. Swirling, the otters seized them. Lut was impressed. The trick might fail on the river, for not all fish fled for cover, but he admired the female's cunning.

She beguiled him. She was wild, a silky savage. He cared for the creature – he had known that at the burrow. Now she prowled with breath bated. 'We're near the lake – watch your step. This is Fingertaker's province.'

'I'm not afraid of the old one.' He eyed the mere. Night had altered its aspect. Reeds were white, willows pallid. They looked deathly and haunted. 'Wait,' Lut said, 'I'll scout forward.'

Alone, he marched without bravado, suspicious of shadows. The reeds murmured. A duck scared him, bursting up from the sedges to fly quacking through moonbeams. He collected his senses. The lake was unruffled. By day, life had swarmed there; now the place was deserted. It shone with chill silver beauty. Lut listened. There was a sigh, a slight stir in the evening.

'Shhhh. . . .'

He crouched low in the herbage. Again he heard the sound, louder. 'Sh-hhh. . . .' Like the wind in an ash tree. The wind had dropped. A grey shape slid above him. It checked, sideslipped, checked again, then dived, banking. With each dive the swish was audible. The heron flattened and glided. Legs down, it spread its air vanes and landed. The bird froze watchfully. For a minute, head tall, it made no movement, then, hunching, paced the shore on stiff stilts.

Lut snorted.

Fingertaker's province! What of that? Lut had fought the giant and lived. Lut had prospered in battle. Before the punt sank, he had bearded the old one. He recalled his jinking sorties, the way he parried; his evasions and lunges. That was just a beginning. The boy had stopped the conflict. Next time, Lut would dazzle, make rings round the marsh lord, destroy his claim to the female. But now, Lut had other interests.

He called back to his companion. Nothing stirred. He could not see her and called again, worried. She could not, he thought, have left him. The fear stabbed, but was banished. He saw the spray rising, the spit from her gallop. Droplets twinkled as she flowed through the shallows to halt where he waited. Together, they plunged into the moonlit lake.

'They will pay,' barked the herons.
    'The bitch belongs to the Marsh Lord.'
    'Who claims his own.'
    The birds hurried. Eggs had hatched; cries for food rocked the treetops. 'Yek-yek-yek!' The noise was deafening.
    Fingertaker ignored it. He had heard worse – the screaming loveplay of otters where kingcups bloomed. The sky had flashed and he had seen the pair sporting. Now the giant prowled the beechwood, an inner storm raging. He had scented the culprits. He moved with stealth.
    'Yek-yek-yek!'
    Nestlings clamoured.
    Fingertaker reached the wood's edge.
    Lut yawned. By the brook he watched idly as Harn fed his offspring and left the nest. Grey sails winnowed. The bitch otter was drowsing. Then, as Harn cleared the beeches, the bird flung a warning, a rasping 'Aak!' and Lut alerted the female.
    'Dive, we're in danger!'
    There was silence. Gullets full, the broods were fleetingly gagged and a rare hush descended. Lut watched the bitch vanish. He paused. The quietness was eerie. There was a ditch beneath the mound and he stood there, nose inquiring. It happened suddenly. The wood's hem opened, he heard a murderous roar, and Fingertaker was charging.
    Downhill the giant thundered, across the ground of the dance-gathering to the ditch, where Lut received him. The impact dazed him.

84

They faced each other.

'She's mine, Fingertaker.'

The monster came again, growling – the broad head a ram which sent Lut reeling backwards.

'Die, Lut!' the giant slavered. 'Die savaged and broken! The bitch is mine!'

With a grunt he crashed forward, hurling Lut to the water. They sank struggling, Fingertaker on top, the sheer bulk of the beast bearing Lut to the bottom where the silt closed above him. He squirmed. Sludge filled his nostrils. Somehow he broke the giant's hold and the two reached the sedges. Their coats were spiked, their snarling heads fierce as tigers'.

'Yek-yek-yek!' screamed the nestlings.

Water sloshing, Lut sallied. An armed paw hurled him sideways. A second blow sent him spinning.

Thrusting back again, he was put down so fiercely that once more he retreated, standing feebly to take Fingertaker's charge at the water's edge. Huge jaws snatched him. Swung and dragged, he felt consciousness ebbing, then broke free, smeared in mucus. An eye was bloody. Through the other he saw his foe's glint of triumph. 'Die, Lut!' The marsh lord lumbered closer. 'Die the death of the ratling!'

Lut inched backwards.

At all events, he must keep moving. The brute was old, he thought grimly. 'Keep moving, Lut, tire him. If you don't move, you're finished.'

He dodged twice, and a third time, rolling clear of his opponent. Trees and reeds swam around him.

'Yek-yek-yek!'

Harn was back with his offspring. The bird squinted downwards. He saw the two otters frozen, mouths agape, and knew the conflict was deadly. Nestlings fed, and he stood watching. Several other birds joined him, necks craned, their crests twitching. The battle resounded, seemed to pulse, through the marshes. The snarling beasts circled. Harn could hear their wild hissing, then the water engulfed them.

The gutter heaved. A sudden wave ran the brook, its crest parting, looming heads armed and streaming.

'Die, Lut!' The giant stabbed. 'Die by the law of the marshes!'

85

Lut backed to the sedges. He stopped. Something sharp had scratched his rump. Easing sideways, he saw the barbed wire around him, the tangled web of an old fence. The rusting coil was screened by bog growth. Wriggling through, Lut crouched trembling. His eyes gleamed. 'You're old, Fingertaker!' His voice came from the fastness. 'The bitch is mine!'

'Lut is shrewd,' crooned the herons.

'Die!' the marsh lord screamed, charging.

Lut listened. The cry turned to anguish. The giant had struck the wire headlong, barging into its meshes where the hidden barbs held him. For a while he was frantic. He lashed and heaved at the obstruction. Then, tense with frustration, the great otter shuddered. Striving now with greater patience, squirming this way and that, he rid himself of the torment. Numb, he shook confusedly.

Lut drove from the flank. Like a bolt he made impact, penetrating the neck hair, the stubborn skin. Fingertaker still quivered. Rearing up, he clawed madly, striping Lut with lacerations. The young otter held on. Thus, had he landed the sea eel, with that same tenacious jawlock. Half blind, he clung fiercely, ignoring his own pain.

'Let us treat,' cried the marsh lord. 'Leave the bitch and go freely.'

'I'm taking her, old one.'

The giant grew frenzied, tail lashing. Flecked with foam, he pitched over and the two beasts rolled snapping – a half-hundredweight furball – once more to the streamlet. Along its brink the fight stormed until, still raging, they toppled, the flow slopping upwards. For a moment they floundered then sank, grappling, to the bottom, the river weed closing. Lut clung like a limpet. Fingertaker was weakening, his struggles less violent. Mud swirled. It made soup of the water, spoiling it for the herons, who saw nothing but bubbles.

'One is drowning,' they croaked.

'One, or both.'

'Their lungs have emptied.'

Lut gasped, breath exhausted. A whisker from triumph, his head was filling with thunder, his chest drawing tighter.

He would be cheated. The giant would escape him. He tried to hang on, pulse drumming, but bright lights were flashing and he kicked feebly upwards. An instant latter he surfaced. He watched the giant reach the sedges.

'Fingertaker. . . .'

Lut was too drained to follow.

Fingertaker glanced back, great head drooping. 'Take the bitch, Lut, she's yours. Leave my marsh realm.'

The man did not believe it – it was a trick of the water, a warp of time. He had boiled the kettle on the grate. Then, while tea brewed, the boatman had partly dressed, filled a mug and blinked through the window at Hunter's woods. The morning star had grown faint and a night-roving badger was heading home. The sow trundled a ball of bedding. She was refurnishing. A thin trail of dropped straws stretched from the barn to the oaks, where she had her set.

He had shaved. It had rained, a spring shower as he fried breakfast, the soft patter in tune with the sizzling pan. He had heard martins that morning and seen the first swallow. The bird had turned on blue pinion then blistered the rain-drops with whiplash curves. In a while the sun had sparkled and the man called the ferry cat. She had not come for her milk and he bawled from the doorstep. A woodpecker answered, its halloo like mad laughter. It was then, catching sight of the jetty, that disbelief seized him.

A tousled figure was fishing. The boatman paused, his eyes narrow. It was a trick of the river. Time had blunted his vision, which was fickle at distance. Yet he could see the float bobbing, the rod aslant from the platform. Scuffling nearer, he noticed the plimsolls. Rooks were roistering. At first their thunder outvoiced him, then, 'You!' he exploded. 'What the hell are *you* doing? What's up? You've no right, ye young beggar!'

'I always fish here.'

The boy reeled in, a small red-finned roach gleaming. He tossed it back. Nearby, the water vole was paddling. The youngster grinned. The vole's snout wrinkled. He looked ill-suited to the river, possessing neither a good rudder not webbed feet, yet the plump beast swam stoutly, as if trotting in the current. When he dived, tiny bubbles festooned him like the scales of a fish. He popped up by a log, where a second vole snuffled. The boy re-cast. 'She's as podgy as he is!' He played the line, laughing. 'Make a good couple.'

'Never mind the blamed creatures!'

The boatman choked. He was still disbelieving. It was a scene out of context, as if nothing had happened; as if nothing had changed. His scowl held the urchin. 'You've no right, boy. You've been nursed and well cared for; now you're back here at daybreak. Playing truant. Don't tell me they know! Don't say they wake in the wee hours and turn you out to go fishing! B'God, if *she* saw you – her from the Welfare – perched out on that jetty. . . .'

'It's not Hunter's.'

'No one said it was Hunter's.'

'Well? *You* never minded.'

The smile returned, bright as the sun in the willows, where bees worked the catkins. 'Maybe not,' huffed the boatman, 'and maybe I should've. There'd be a punt on that bank if I'd minded.' And he would owe the Hall nothing. The debt to Hunter rankled. Ragged grey clouds were drifting beneath towering white anvils. The rape had turned garish yellow. The man eyed the coverts. Matted boughs of oak jutted, jostling yet leafless ash poles. But the thorn hems had coloured, and he traced Hunter's drive by the greening of May and the memory of a visit made only for the boy's sake. The lad had caused enough trouble. 'We'd have a punt still,' he rumbled.

The boy shrugged. 'She let water.'

'You discovered!'

'I never saw what done for her. She sank in the canal.'

'We know what happened.'

'One more day, I'd have got there.' The child sighed, his tone solemn. 'I'd have reached the old herons, found the brook by the beeches. Lut will get there. He'll find a mate like the vole has; bring her back with him.'

'They go, son. They don't come back.'

'Bet? I'd bet my rod and tackle!'

The boy's smile was certain. The vale in spring was compelling. Small fish frisked in the freshets, the rock grew warm. Now the tide of growth welled and great bees lurched by bluebells. 'He'll come back,' the boy blurted. 'Wind and ice wouldn't stop him. He just romped in the thunder. Heck,' he cried, 'I wish you had seen him. He'll return, all right.'

There was a splash. The voles had dived, heading upstream. Boughs of sycamore drew them. They liked none better than the young leaves of sycamore, reached from the strand where they landed, shedding droplets. Standing tall, the voles plucked at low branches, rolled the leaves into tubes then sat upright and guzzled. The boy dangled his legs. 'A pair of otters!' He beamed. 'The old holt will be full. There'll be cubs. We'll have a real otter stream, like it used to be.'

'Bah!' The man grunted. You could tell the lad nothing. 'Just be glad you're alive. Drat the beasts, they got you into the mess. Me and Hunter dragged you out; it was us who traipsed the ditches. Be thankful, boy.'

'I came to thank you – you and Hunter.'

'Watch your step,' said the boatman. He viewed the Hall through the oak crowns. 'Mind your manners with that ogre or you'll land in the dungeons. I'd come with you,' he vouchsafed, 'but I can't leave the ferry. Demands o' duty.' He looked sheepish. 'You watch your step with that blamed tyrant.'

The Hall towered before him. It was grimmer than he had thought, more improbably massive. He seemed to shrink in its presence. Stone-framed windows stared blankly. As he watched, a jackdaw pitched to a chimney and dropped inside.

90

The boy crept to the back. The front terrace lacked cover. He feared the mullioned glare from unseen chambers, less awed at the rear where dustbins stood in the yards and there were places to duck into. He stole forward. Doors hung on warped hinges: doors to sheds, stables, tack rooms. They leaked fusty odours. He passed long-empty kennels. There was a reek of disinfectant then a tiled passage beckoned and, sniffing, he slipped inside. He could hear footsteps. Drawing back, he saw the crone in the doorway. 'Yes, my dear?'

She bore her broom like a halberd. 'Someone wants to see Hunter?' The old cleaner cackled. 'Well, that's nice. That'll make a nice change, dear.'

'To thank him.'

'I see. Well, I'll take you along, for he'll be in the study.'

She led the way through dim regions, feet shuffling, tapping faintly with the broomstick, and the boy's disquiet mounted. Drab corridors twisted ahead. He glimpsed strange musty closets, great oak-panelled caverns where powder fell from the minings of woodworms. Soon his bearings escaped him. He felt each step now a hazard. Something on the wall rapped him: the hilt of a sword. Other weapons hung near, huge and rusting. Above them, heads jutted, skins ravaged by mites, dusty webs on the antlers. The urchin's gut tightened. Then a stout door was opening and the desk stood ahead, a vast parapet cluttered with debris, behind which the man was bent like a trench soldier under fire. 'What's that brat doing, woman?' There was scarcely a movement.

'Go in, dear,' the crone said. 'A young man to see Hunter.'

The boy's gaze roamed in terror. Hulking furniture flanked him, dour oaken escarpments, and he heard the hound snoring. It was eerie, oppressive. He saw dull glass-domed birds, their defunct plumage faded, and a pike in a showcase, big-headed and leery. He smelled the stale dusty violence of stuffed ermine and goshawk.

'Out!' The man looked up fiercely.

'Take no notice,' the crone said. 'You go on, dear, and thank him.'

But the boy had stopped, speechless. The otter heads petrified him. Hung in rows, they gaped drily, their painted tongues parched, the mouths twisted, glass eyes in rifled sockets – the lost fishers of the stream, Lut's ancestors and kindred. Lut's dam could be nailed there; his brothers and sisters. Scenes from hell had been framed there, beasts impaled on barbed tridents. Men grinned from the pictures. The boy swallowed grimly. His nails were searing his palms and he swung round, tears scalding, fists smooth as stream pebbles. 'You killed them!' he shouted. 'You done for the otters! You murdered them!'

'Don't you mind the old heads, dear. . . .'

'He killed them!'

The wizened woman clucked hoarsely.

Hunter slammed the door on her. 'Enough noise, boy. Who sent you? That damned fool from the ferry?'

'No one sent me.'

'You've no right to be up here.'

'You killed them!'

'Sit down and stop bawling.'

'Let me out!'

'Silence, damn you!' It was roared, Hunter's haggard face livid. His frame was shaking. Arm outstretched, he stepped nearer and the boy recoiled, glowering. The reaching hand drew towards him, large and rough, the skin scaly, the forefinger missing. He had felt it at the millpond, bearing down on his shoulder. Now he dodged, his fists forward. He was trembling, but rage surpassed the lad's fear and he snarled with defiance, 'You shan't kill me! Don't touch me!'

'Heaven's, man!' Hunter shrugged. The child was like a wild creature. 'We didn't save you to *kill* you.'

'You murdered the otters.'

Hunter limped to the window. He saw deer move and vanish. For a space he said nothing, then turned, his voice rasping. 'They were poisoned. Poison wiped out the otters: pesticides used in farming. In just two years.' He prowled the floor, haunted. 'For centuries otters were hunted; it didn't threaten the species. The beasts were plentiful. They were poisoned – the whole lot in two years by toxic chemicals.'

'You killed otters. You're making excuses. You harried them.'

'Don't question my life, boy! You know nothing. How can you? A truant and boat thief! Times have changed: things were different.' The man returned to the desk, sitting stiffly there, grey-faced. He had drained himself for his deerlands, for his coverts and gamebanks; become a penniless recluse. They kept making him offers. He shuffled the papers. Brash men with brash millions who had plans for his acres. They would bring in their chainsaws, clear the banks, spray the reedbeds. They would grub out and poison, make the valley 'efficient'. If he sold. Hunter's fist slammed the desk. 'Don't you dare accuse *me*, boy. If I sold, the vale would perish. Not just otters – all wildlife.'

The boy eyed the gargoyles. The man's talk was evasive.

Hunter snarled, 'You know nothing.'

'I know you killed them – the otters.'

'Come here.'

The lad held his ground, watchful.

Hunter said, 'I'm no monster. You've been listening to tales, to that fool of a boatman. The fool peasant's senile.'

'You killed otters!'

'By God, you're persistent!' The ramrod spine weakened. 'It's done with; it's history. How the deuce would a brat know? Times were different, I tell you. D'you think I'd still hunt 'em – that I don't wish 'em back?' He gave a short, savage whinny. 'D'you think I don't have regrets, boy? What I needn't put up with is puppy insolence. Damn your yammering!'

The cleaning woman re-entered. She brought a tray.

Hunter snarled, 'Give him coffee. Pass that bottle across, boy.'

The boy went to the sideboard. His gaze was guarded, still on the old otter-hunter. 'You mean, you wouldn't harm Lut?'

'Lut?' The man tipped the bottle.

'The otter.'

Hunter's cowled eyes showed interest. 'Harm Lut?' he said, glinting. 'I'll make a pact. But play *your* part. If he returns, I'll not harm him.' He gave a flicker of triumph. 'Go back where you came from and no more absconding, no more playing the truant. You do that, it's a bargain.'

The urchin frowned gravely. He saw no cause to trust Hunter. The obscene masks condemned him. The man was old, mad and cunning: as deep as a pike pool. As darkly treacherous.

'Agreed, boy?'

The boy thought of the otter.

'Agreed,' he lied.

The otters swam at a fathom in marbled water. They had slipped to sea from the brook, sporting boisterously in the breakers and amid rocky outcrops, hunting crustaceans. At the tideline they cracked razorshells and crabs while sandflies hopped on the bubble wrack. Beneath the waves, the pair glided, Lut leading the female. The sun was brilliant. Bronzed by it, their long languid shapes seemed to celebrate freedom – perhaps from the old one, whose spell Lut had broken.

His urge to leave, now, was strong. The bitch was free to go with him to the river where blue duns would be stirring, the scent of sallow powerful. Trout, recouping from winter, would be guzzling frog and chub spawn; spates and peaty pools, warming. The old holt called to Lut. Its sycamore would be unfurling, earthen banks fresh and minty. In his mind the stream fluttered, its water claws rippling where the big grey slab jutted and spring's sunbeams twinkled.

But the bitch was uncertain. 'The river's forbidden. Otters fled it to exile. It's dangerous, Lut.'

'We first met by the river.'

'The broad stream is alluring but I'm marsh-born. I'm afraid of the valley.'

'I live there.'

'Just you, Lut.'

'The more room for both of us!' In swims vibrant with fry, flanked by trefoil-leaved sorrel beneath Hunter's woodlands; on banks browsed by quiet cattle and lively with wagtails. How could Lut convey the valley? Once an artist had stopped there, held at dusk by a greenness so luminous it coloured the sky itself. He could not paint it; it was a scene beyond description. It lived in Lut's soul. The beast could smell and hear the reaches but his nostalgia had no power to sway others.

Now his search swept the seabed. The otters were hungry. A smudge of sandgrains caught his interest, a small flurry betraying the flounder despite its camouflaged skin, and the fisher manoeuvred. His prey was broad-backed and chary. Discovered, the flounder decamped, sand wake billowing. Lut fired himself downwards. Legs tucked back, he harpooned through bright water, eyes fixed on his target, feet splaying at impact. In gritty clouds he swirled twice, the fish flapping. It was dead as he looped back to his companion. Proudly, Lut swam around her, the meaty prize flaunted, then made a rare gesture. Releasing the flatfish, he let it drift towards the female.

With a flip, she drew backwards. The other's kill was inviolable. No wild law was more hallowed and she withdrew from the flounder. Lut batted it to her. The bitch otter's eyes questioned. Again, the male biffed his catch in her direction, veering off with feigned disinterest, and now she nosed the fish slyly. Her grab was swift, her rush for shore spurred by guilt. But Lut's delight was emphatic. Making circles on the beach, he flopped near while she feasted, churring happily.

'Lut,' she belched when she had gorged, 'I've been thinking. . . .' They *had* met by the river. It *was* his home. And they *would* be alone there.

The dog otter strutted. 'Have no fear,' said the swagger, 'trust Lut, who killed the sea eel and is Fingertaker's equal. You'll be safe with him.'

Soon after, they set off together by Jury's Gut. The channel led inland to the dyke called White Kemp, which in turn crossed the grazings towards the canal where the punt had sunk. The marsh dome dazzled. An early grass snake, awakened by the sun, crossed their front, yellow throat above water; midge and fly hatches shimmered. The otters paddled abreast. For each of them company was a novel experience, and they glanced one at the other, from time to time, as if dreaming, occasionally touching. Then they would dive, the reeds would quake and they would rise in playful battle.

It was a fair voyage. Suddenly, in the way each year it happens, small songbirds filled the sedges and the first marsh frogs cackled. Sturdy lambs watched the travellers, frisking back from the dyke banks, ewes stamping their forefeet. An eye glared from a burrow: the chestnut-hooped shelduck, already deep-nested. Self-absorbed, the otters took little interest. Lut cavorted. The lithe female entranced him.

Only once did he leave her: when they came to the marsh church. Then, while the bitch idled, he slipped out from the sedges and made for the building. It seemed less bleak in the sunshine, small roof warmly lichened, its moat and reedy environs alive with birds and beasts. Sheep lay close to the walls, swans preening near them. Skylarks marked out their stations. A cuckoo called.

As the otter went forward, a sandy hare left a hollow and loped slowly around the building, its black-tipped ears twitching. Wading birds probed soggy dips in the pasture. The last time Lut had stood there the boy had been with him, the night wild, the place desolate. Now a tranquil congregation browsed and sunned by the structure, reassured by human absence. Lut ran quickly to the entrance. The wooden door balked him and, standing up, two paws on the obstruction, he sniffed searchingly.

The smaller otter snoozed quietly. It was safe in the sedges and she lay, four legs upwards, drying a pale stomach, her loose coat creased beside her in velvet folds. A large fly made her restless. Rolling over, she looked vainly for Lut, her nose brisk in the reed stems. There was earth on her shoulders.

With a squirm, she shrugged it off, growing impatient. At first her growl was a hum, low and waspish, becoming higher as she chafed until an angry wail left her, an imperative summons.

Lut heard and glanced back. But curiosity kept him, a vague allegiance to the past, while he smelled the step and doorpost. At length, no trace of the boy there, he turned away, interest flagging. The more urgent tie drew him. She was out of the dyke, crouched in wait, her eyes flashing. Moments later they romped, but her greeting nip smarted. It was fiercer than a welcome – a possessive reminder of loyalty due.

They saw the vale from the wharf. Orchards blossomed and Lut whistled his pleasure. Ahead ranged the old haunts, his home swims and reaches. Nearby stood the bothy. Soon the jetty would loom, the cottage beside it. Soon they would see the rusty lean-to and the gnarled cider apple. He would show the bitch marvels: rooty banks arched with grasses, unguessed pathways through spinneys, long gurgling culverts. There was a fallen tree to delight her, hollowed out and made to snooze in. There were alleys and runnels; pools where fish almost begged to be captured.

Two points crossed his mind. 'Stay away from the farm pond; the wall-eyed lurcher is dangerous. And keep clear of Hunter.'

Beyond that, he promised nothing but gladness – otter country. The rock stood to prove it, testifying their title by ancient lineage. But the bitch had stopped doubting. The chanting flow, its hymnal lilt, had enslaved her. It was the season of elvers and the bright morsels thrilled her. In seething swarms they toiled upstream, blindly seeking new homes. Navigating by water pressure, the dwarf eels thrust at currents with a wriggling compulsion which drew them to rills and ditches in thousands. Where drainage gushed, they drove at it. Rocks and dams did not stop them. In squirming queues they formed iridescent ribbons up pouring weirs.

Hundreds threshed below the wharf, trying hard to climb the wall where a pipe discharged. The bitch scooped them with glee, plucking them from the bulwark, treading water as she guzzled. Her face beamed as she chomped them. This indeed was abundance, and her relish was gluttonous. Lut enjoyed her gutsy rapture. It bode well as they came to the vale that her mood should be blissful. Eventually, bloated, the female lay by the stream and watched Lut build a mud slide.

Several times he climbed the steep earthen bank, smoothing the slope as he descended, until the chute glistened. Then, lubricated by water, he pushed off at the top on a test run. Lut zipped down like a bomb. Disappearing in spume, he bounced up, a jester, showing off on the surface. The other chirped her approval. Quick to try out the slide, she scarcely ruffled the stream as she cleaved it. Together, the otters stroked for the bank, forefeet pumping, and Lut gave way as they jostled to slide again.

'Like this, Lut! Come on down; try to catch me!'

Down through fronds of vegetation in pursuit of the slim torpedo. Up, to caper like dolphins. For half an hour the pair sported, sliding, chasing and wrestling. As they tired, they played less energetically, juggling sticks in the water, and other floating objects. Lut lay back on the river, a twig clasped in his fingers. Idly drifting, he gazed at the heavens, applauding his achievement, the return of the campaigner. He wished Harn could see him. Prince of poachers! What a triumph! What a prize he had brought from the marshes! Paddling smugly ashore, he climbed onto the wharf and cast around for the female.

Elvers frothed on the surface. For a while she was absent, exploring underwater, and Lut thought of wooded reaches, the millpond. He would show her the rapids, the white teeth of the river, and a bank where frogs sunned like crickets. He would take her to cress beds, to cool arbours. Peering down the knife-edge between the wharf and the hustling flood, he imagined her wonder on reaching the vale from her muddy brook.

'Lut!'

He looked puzzled.

She had come up, her squeal angry. Spluttering, she peered into the depths then back at the dog otter. Her face was furious. It said, 'You never warned me of *this*. You let me plunge without warning. Don't just stand there, do something!'

Lut joined her. Already, she was diving, commanding attendance, and he followed her steeply beside the wharf's slime-daubed bulwark. The flow ran deep there, its streaming vaults shadowed. He trailed the bubbles she sloughed, thrusting into the chasm. Thongs of miry weed grappled them. Ahead, the small bitch sank dimly, with sinuous movements, through the thickening murk. They were ghosting past silt dunes, sunken coombes. Craggy stones loomed and a strange cagelike structure: an old iron-framed bedstead. Lut swam bemusedly. There was gloom on the bottom, lowly snail-life and bivalves, but no danger he knew of.

The leading otter banked sharply. Now she cruised with more caution, allowing Lut to draw closer. Head to tail, the beasts volplaned. The bitch twisted, eyes searching, then abruptly backpaddled and Lut tuned to the vibrations. Fins were winnowing. They were large fins. Turning, he saw the cavern and, darkly in the ingress, the monstrous pike watching. The pike, Esox, was daunting. His great lower lip jutted. Bands of teeth made a trap of his mouth, the barbs set backwards, attached not only to his jaws but his tongue as well. He was as long as an otter and leered now with malice.

Lut's eyes twinkled. He knew Esox of old; they had reached an accommodation, a truce of mutual convenience, but the pike's gaze was frosty. 'Keep her out of it, otter. She has no right on these reaches. Our pact is exclusive.'

'*Was*, Esox. Things are going to be different.'

'By what law? Bream, grayling and trout – the fishing's mine here.'

Lut blew air with derision. 'The law of *Lut*, Esox! The law that routed the old one and vanquished the conger! Note the law with care, Esox, for things have changed. You stay merely on sufferance.'

The bitch's instincts were fiercer. She saw the broad-banded flanks and cruel jaw of the pike and felt a stabbing revulsion. Lut might tolerate Esox; her hatred was steadfast. She inched nearer the monster and Lut dived between them. 'He must go, Lut. Remove him!' But the pike was not waiting. Rayed tail flicking, he slouched off downriver, too

100

shrewd to take risks, yet cursing the otters. The bitch would hear from him. Let her spawn. The river shark could be patient. Let her brood come to water. . . .

'He won't touch you,' Lut promised.

'Maybe not.'

The bitch glared down the current. She did not fear for herself. Like her abnormal hunger, it was something else.

A thin call!

The boy was sure he had heard it, skirling up through the vale from the distant flats. But the sound was deceptive; it might have come from much closer, Stone Bridge or the ferry. Or have been an illusion, for the evening was still and full of a curious resonance. Noises hung where mist was creeping; sounds skipped on the millpond. Near the pool, the boy listened.

The mill creaked and gurgled. Small fish nudged the surface, and once, when he moved, the whole shoal dived as one, with a splash like water thrown from a bucket. It was a place of strange moods, the misty slack by the big wheel, and all sounds there were suspect. 'Lut?' The urchin turned quickly. A crow had perched in a thorn tree. The bird nibbled a claw, surveying him darkly. But the call had trailed feebly. 'That's not you, is it, Lutra?'

A bat was hawking. Soon others would join it, emerging from the mill house. Eerie noises abounded despite the smooth water, odd bubblings and boilings, as if the pool was haunted. Men had ended their lives there. According to the boatman, all such mills had their ghosts, grim histories of drownings, of debt-riddled millers, or those simply bewitched by the secret depths. The boy shuddered. The place scared him, but he was sure Lut would come there when he returned.

Unwrapping a chocolate bar, the youngster munched. He thought of the kitchen at Ferry Cottage. His belly rumbled, but he dared not go to the jetty. From now on he was in hiding, his Otter Watch known to nobody. Except, he mused, the dusky crow in the thorn; and the crow told no tales, as much alone as the urchin. To the boy he was Corbie – Black Corbie, a skulking bachelor, the so-called 'third bird' of crow territory. Now Corbie's wings flexed and he coughed a low warning, a deep-throated 'Krrr!'

The lad started. There was a movement in the woods. As Corbie fled, the boy ducked into the mill. Someone came through the birch poles and the boy, still retreating, crouched at length in deep shadows, old joists ranged above him, the floor thick with debris. Age-old cogwheels stood idle, great pulleys were dust-clogged. Between their arthritic spindles stretched cobwebs so dense they might have been canvas, the sails of some ancient coal barge, as they flapped at his shoulders. The mill groaned like a sailship. Across the darkness a square of light marked a window. Where glass remained in the casement, filth obscured the boy's vision, but a pane had been broken. He peered through the opening.

It looked out on the pond and the wood's scrubby fringes. Hunter loomed from the trees. Slowly he came down the mill path, his staff lashing at brambles, until he stood by the water. The boy watched apprehensively – he had crushed the grass where he had been waiting. He only hoped Hunter missed it, for the man was a bloodhound. But the head scarcely turned, and it seemed to the urchin the gaunt figure was concerned with the pool's depths and little else. So long did Hunter pause that the boy grew stiff from not moving. Perhaps the man would jump in, drown himself like the millers.

The boy did not want to watch. He felt a pang of compassion. What if the madman had meant it, was truly remorseful? He had his virtues – spared the land, preserved the cover. He can't drown, thought the urchin, whatever he once did! The lad looked away. When next he peeped the other still had not moved and he lost sympathy. *He's after Lut!* The thought uncurled like a viper. *I don't trust him. He's waiting like I am.*

Across the trees the crow circled. The boy saw the black prowler and wished he had Corbie's wings, the power to spot Lut and warn him. The only way to do that was to get below the pool, on the bank of the stream; and when Hunter did not shift, the boy slipped tensely from the window.

His steps were muffled. Dust as thick as a rug forsook years of inertia and he fought back a sneeze, clawing webs from his eyebrows. His shins rapped an obstacle. Part of the floor above had fallen and a misplaced board brought the boy to his knees, where he paused, the wince of pain frozen, afraid he might have been heard. For a minute he knelt there, unnerved by the creaking. Outside, the wheel jerked, a token of history which strained the mill's timbers. Then, once more, the boy was ducking between cumbersome engines, his ears alert. Midges danced in the door and he hugged the jamb. He whistled in relief. The man had gone.

In the west the sky smouldered. It ruddied the pond mist and turned the stream crimson. The boy rubbed his hands. 'Come on, Lut, it's all ours. He's gone back to his dungeons!' The dying day lingered. He eyed the quiet valley. It was his world; he felt right there. The boy knew its creatures, understood their sly shyness, the peace and violence of the river and shading woods. He felt the harmony of nature, most awesome as dusk fell. Then came the scream of the rabbit, which told that stoats hunted, and the notes of the songthrush; then the waltzing hare twirled and the owl peddled slaughter. The boy could hear his pulse beating.

Rooks homed, a small party. He watched their flight by the sun-fire. The blazing vale darkened. A great perfume was spreading from countless May blossoms. Everywhere, they glowed warmly, joined by crowns of cow parsley in lustrous galaxies. The boy gulped the fragrance. The pool was still and he moved around its rim until he found the man's footmarks. A tingling prescience gripped him. He felt the closeness of the otter, yet could have offered no evidence why – until the water burst upwards and a head and neck glistened.

'Lut. . . .' He choked back the welcome.

A second head had arisen, somewhat smaller than the first, and he gawped, his face shining. He wished to shout, to cavort with excitement, for Lut had brought back a partner, but the lad feared to scare her. Instead, he watched dumbly. A slight chill fluttered through him, produced by emotion, and he felt his eyes pricking. The beasts bobbed, streaming water. They were wild in the twilight, primeval as the pond mist which drifted over them. For a moment he lost them, then the female had landed.

103

She sniffed the grass, shaking briskly, her silver bib shining. She was perfect, the boy deemed – sleek and savagely lovely. Where she stood, bugle blossomed, the small blue flowers pressed against her. She was pretty as bugle. 'Lut and Bugle,' he muttered. It rang true, a swift christening. 'Bugle's cubs. . . .' he tried quietly. He was trembling. It could happen. Otter cubs could be born on the stream again.

The holt was dry. Deep in the bank, the clay walls were familiar. It was the most private place Lut knew and he led the way proudly. The bitch had paused on the strand. Taking stock, she had approved the location, then followed into the tunnel. The male could hear her behind him. Head low, he nosed the darkness, turned a corner and bristled. Small eyes pricked in the gloom, stabbed at him viciously.

Lut huffed. There was a scuffle and several shapes fled the chamber, retreating through the back tunnel. This emerged above the bank, where drooping boughs met tall grasses and, as Lut pushed his head out, he saw the rats ranged before him. It was raining. The rain gusted, shaking layered leaves of sycamore and damping the grey-coated rodents. The rats formed a half circle. Hunched and insolent, they reminded Lut of the day he had sprawled bleeding and helpless, and the rat pack had slavered. He snarled grimly.

The holt was hallowed. He had grown up there, brought his mate to its closets. The rodents defiled it. They had made free in his absence and now he swore, hissed like the swift, adjacent water. The rat leader scorned him. A scrawny sow, she sat up on thick-docked tail and quizzed the otter, her spine humped. She was as cunning as Esox, eyes mean, and where the horny legs ended her bare fingers were claw-tipped. Curling her nose, she showed incisors like chisels in yellow pairs. Lut sallied, but the rodent was agile, scuttling to safety. At that, the rats retired.

They left their reek in his nostrils and he went below, ruffled. The bitch was in the chamber. Plainly, Bugle was delighted, scratching, scraping and turning in circles. Her soft grunting was soothing, a homely echo of cubhood, and Lut forgot the intruders. There was no room for him to share her house chores, and he doubted she would thank him. Instead, he lay in the outer gallery, enjoying her pleasure. Yet, he thought, it lacked something, for at length she grew restless, dissatisfied with the litter, which was old now and rat-soiled. He went outside.

The rain swept in bright curtains. Mosquitoes were whining. Lut paused thoughtfully then, resolved, bustled into the wood, heading up the slope. Thorn and bramble engulfed him, and lean tossing poles, starved of light between the oak trees. The place was a jungle. Some poles had fallen, stripped of bark by birds and squirrels as they leaned at crazy angles. Thickets straggled. Thanks to Hunter, neglect had spawned a wild magic, a tangled, untrammelled beauty, steeped in mystery. Lut thrilled to the wildwood.

In its depths there were hideouts, dark recesses of hedgehogs and the deep pipes of badgers. Jays screamed and 'pies chattered. Below, unobserved, the dunnock brooded her blue eggs. Few wood-dwellers were conspicuous. Lut knew most by their signs: print of fox, slot of deer, the plucked fur of a rabbit whose nest was near. He heard the chink now of goldcrests, small birds in moist boughs, and smelled the dank, secret cloisters. Once, he had found a skull amid that tangle, bleached and resting on sarsen, wreathed in ground-trailing ivy. It conjured no beast of Lut's world. He had lingered to marvel. Sometimes he just stood and listened. Sounds crooned through the columns: the far sigh of water, a tractor trundling the plough swell.

A breeze rocked the treetops. In the squall, whippy poles clashed and the canopy opened. Lut followed the badgers' path. He was not the first. Where Brock made his roadways, bulldozing the herbage, many small mammals roved, as their spore proclaimed. Tall boughs clattered. Lut scurried, passing fuants of badger, cupped in shallow latrines. Branches squeaked. Then a vast field of digging marked the roof of the set. It was old, some holes dark and subsiding; others raw, the tilth ruddy. Down below, the boar snuffled. He would not rise until nightfall and Lut went by boldly.

He did not stop until he reached the wood's topside, spying cautiously. The rain was over. Where cloud remained it was sparse and the sun flashed on bushes. He peered forward. Deer were browsing near the Hall. There was a rich smell of earth and, just out from the covert, a bank of ferns glistened. They were the best ferns Lut knew, broad and soft. Moments later he held a spray of the growth tightly in his teeth.

Back through the wood, his pace quickened. The trees were suddenly still, the muffled roar of wind gone, his journey downhill. Droplets twinkled. As he ran, the ferns fluttered so his appearance was coquettish, until, reaching the holt, he dragged them awkwardly inside. Bugle's pleasure was poignant. Pouncing on the fresh bedding, she shoved it here and there, purring. There seemed no end to her fussing but at last she was suited. Lut left her. Fangs glinting, he swam with self-satisfaction to Otter Rock.

'Lut!'

He glimpsed the boy in the rushes.

'You made it.' The lad bobbed with excitement. 'I've seen her, Lut. She's a picture.'

Far off, a dog blethered.

The otter froze. His dark eyes quizzed the urchin. There was no surprise in them – only pleasure and a mild reservation. He glanced quickly at the holt.

'Come on, Lut, I'll not disturb her! Heck, she'll soon get to know me when she sees that we're pals. I'm on watch to protect her. Don't forget we're old shipmates.'

He stopped at Hunter's boathouse. For a while he eyed the clear shallows, his countenance shifty. A stickleback fanned there, the red-throated cock fish, spines ready for battle, fiercely guarding the nest where the hen had spawned. The boy sidled to the shed. He could see the dinghy inside, but on trying the doors, found them locked. Frustrated, he sloped upstream seeking Lut, who had taken to hunting above the mill.

The bitch was touchy now, moody. Her fullness showed. The last time the boy glimpsed her, Bugle's belly had scraped the shingle, and he knew his prayers answered. He had pleaded in the marsh church and this was the outcome: a miracle on the river – except, he quibbled, that true miracles were prompt. Bugle kept the world waiting. She hogged the holt while Lut rambled, and the boy sometimes joined him.

A boat would have helped. They could have fished from the dinghy, sailed past obstacles. On foot, things were harder. The bank was scrubby and thistled, so overgrown in some places that the lad had to wade. But the air was warm. Above the mill the stream narrowed. Spraint was fresh on a boulder. Somewhere, Lut would be lurking, perhaps asleep in the sun, for he liked the green upper reaches.

An otter river! It *had* been, before the brown fishers vanished; would be again, the boy dreamed. He was sure now; sure as the bulge in Bugle's belly. Frogs dived and a swan left her castle. There was one egg there, a monster. Fish fled as he meandered, their shadows bolting like arrows. Several times he called the otter but the stream was unruffled and, where it crossed open meadows, the boy at length rested. Beside a pool was a plank bridge. He sat on it.

Lut sometimes swam there. Now the boy dipped a foot. He had known the water much colder and, stripping, pinched his nose and leaped outwards, legs flailing. The splash resounded. Skin aglow, the lad wallowed, kicking up weedy fountains. He bobbed a minute, his mouth spouting. Hair slicked his forehead. As his eyes cleared, he chuckled. The pool was circled by steers, great inquisitive saps, broad heads skewbald, mesmerized by his antics. Ogling, they pawed dust, pulling back when he splashed, then returning good-humouredly.

For a time he played to a spellbound audience – but eventually its interest was divided. Lut had surfaced and was staging his own act, a twirling, tumbling diversion. 'Still showing off!' the boy spluttered. 'Still a clown, you brown savage!' He chortled with pleasure. Still the Lut of their punt days, obliging when it pleased him! The boy dived, his feet threshing. He saw the sleek form swirl past, then Lut had turned, somersaulting, their bubble trails merging. The boy reached out underwater. For an instant he touched the otter, but the beast was quicksilver, gone with a flash – to stream back, his flanks gleaming.

Above water, they idled. The breath of beeves roofed the river. Like the banks, it was pungent, at once acrid and honeyed. Vetch straggled; new reeds screened the old corpses. The urchin envied the otter. The beast plunged without effort. He made the boy, when he followed, feel clumsy, yet the deep chase was thrilling. The ghosting shape swam alongside. Hair awash, the lad goggled. The creature's closeness excited him, but the child was not deluded. Lut would rather be with Bugle. The boy owed the occasion to her present solitary mood.

He bobbed up, treading water.

She was hard on her partner. 'Never mind,' he gasped, grinning, 'it can't be much longer. Bear up, Lut, I'm with you!' He climbed out, rubbing down with his T-shirt. The steers had stampeded. 'She's here, that's what matters. The main thing is her safety.' To stand guard, maintain watch on the hideout. He frowned suddenly. 'I'm going back,' he decided. He was neglecting his duty. 'Are you coming, Lut?'

Lut regarded him blankly. The beast was not in a hurry. He had little say in the holt now. The last time he tried to enter, the bitch had flown at him, raging, and Lut had left, hurt and puzzled. He eyed the boy's dwindling figure.

'All right, don't!' it called peevishly.

Back at the rock, the boy pondered. Lut seemed awed by the tunnel. Was Bugle still in there? He had not seen her leave. The lad had watched but she had missed normal outings and he feared she had sickened. Until then she had been hungry, a regular hunter. He contemplated the strand. It was deserted. Concerned, he lay prone beneath the tree, easing forward on his elbows until he reached the holt's rear shaft. He put an ear to it. What he heard was not Bugle, the sound was too feeble, the faintest of squeaking, but it

109

banished his foreboding. Almost bursting, he crawled away, sprang to his feet and ran leaping along the bank.

'Lut!' The words burbled from him. 'The cubs have come, Lut. I heard them! It's happened, for Pete's sake. The cubs are here!'

Bugle listened. She did not move, save for cocking an ear, but lay half curled in the darkness, the cubs against her stomach. They were three, wrapped in soft pale grey fur, eyes invisible. For another month they would not lift their heads. Four weeks later, she would wean them. Otter cubs were slow starters. Now, sightless and drowsy, they whimpered as they nestled. Alert, the bitch listened, as ferociously caring as they were vulnerable.

Sounds from outside told stories. She heard the boy go. Birds chattered. Their language was anxious. Blackbirds chinked, their note cautionary, changing swiftly to the *si*-call of terror. Again, she tensed. Then the songsters trilled freely. A hawk had passed over. She nuzzled her infants. Soon the moorhen was clucking, causing greater apprehension, for the fowl spoke of prowlers and the bitch could hear scuffling.

She lay still, her ears straining. The sound came from the rear shaft, a noise like earth falling, or so it seemed in the first place. When it shifted, rasping, scraping in the gallery, she crouched over her young ones. Feet were pattering. She watched the mouth of the chamber. In the gloom, shapes were moving and the smell of rats reached her. It grew thicker. Coarse necks were stretching forward. The otter bitch smouldered.

They incensed her. The rats were audacious, obscene in their impertinence. Bugle's fury exploded. She charged suddenly. The lunge would have startled a man, and the rodents, scrambling backwards, fled in confusion. The rout was shadowy. Claws scampered, voices squealed, rats climbed one on another as the otter pursued them.

Missing her warmth, the cubs grizzled. They were alone and, while she cleared the rear tunnel, danger switched to the front, where the holt was unguarded. Some of the rats had come that way, winding up through the tree roots. The leader paused. The velvet bundles were helpless. With a

110

grunt, the rat sniffed them. She slavered. Others, watching, surged forward. They were thick in the chamber when Lut arrived.

Bursting in from the river, he snatched the nearest, broke its neck and grabbed a second. He felt its spine snap and dropped it. The next he swung at the roof, letting go as it crumpled, to seize a fourth and despatch it. Lut cast around like a terrier. The scrawny leader had escaped. Two of her clan, seeking refuge in the back shaft, found Bugle returning and, trapped between otters, were slaughtered. At that, Lut nosed his offspring. They were unharmed, the small trio affecting. Moved, the dog nudged them fondly.

The female was bristling.

'Stay close, Lut.' The tone belied her hackles. 'Don't go far,' Bugle told him, 'for the cubs and I need you. Stay close to us.'

The mink climbed from the channel, sitting up on the bank where a rabbit had tunnelled. The stars shone on her mantle. It was black, dense with water, bushing out when she shook, though still damp at the throat. She watched the otter approach. Before, the mink would have fled. Now she sniffed with derision, noting his laboured strokes. Fingertaker was ailing. Once, beasts feared his footsteps. Now the mink by the tidegate merely stretched with indifference. Rolling, she dried her neck on the loose diggings.

Fingertaker submerged. He had lost the speed to pursue her. His decline had come quickly, first enfeebling him on land, then impairing his swimming. A bream swung above him. Its deep brassy flanks shimmered. It was a gift for the taking but the old otter faltered, kicking weakly and too late. With a start the fish slipped him, batting back to its kindred. The shoal had gone when he turned and, leaving the water, he was forced to grub for his supper, rootling like a hedgehog.

Grunting, the mink ducked into the bury. The otter's plight did not move her. When the marsh otter perished, his small cousin would fish unrivalled. In the hole, she nosed the bones of a rabbit she had eaten.

The larger beast snarled. It was the snarl of the afflicted, a fierce gesture of foreboding as the otter limped on, now dragging back to the water, where his bow-wake was torpid. At the lock, the keeper's wife saw him briefly. She thought him oddly incautious, swimming full in the starlight. She turned back to the cottage. 'He looked sick,' she told her husband, 'slow and dull. It was him, the big otter.'

'He's old,' the man told her, 'his days are numbered, poor beggar.'

In the trees, herons muttered.

'He'll die,' said the young ones.

'Just an otter.'

'More than that,' Harn corrected. 'At one time he was famous: as famed as Harn is sagacious.'

'Fingertaker? Whose finger did he take, Harn?'

'He took Hunter's.'

Long ago. Now the moon ringed the treetops and Harn cast his mind back. All afternoon hounds had hunted as the otter had doubled, heaved through pools and by thickets – had passed sallow and alder, gasped where willow herb blossomed – until he turned by the rock. Time and again he had dived, lungs bursting. Then, half drowned, he had stood, mouth gaping, as the pack fell on him. Limp and torn, he had drifted, but as the man stooped to claim him, the otter had snapped.

'Seized a finger,' the young herons prompted. 'We'd have taken an eye.'

'Because your instincts are avian.'

'He was stubborn.'

'Would not give up.'

'Tell us more, Harn.'

But the old bird was nodding. Two months after hatching, the young were fledged, full of zest. Harn was weary. It had been long ago. Fingertaker had escaped, joined and ruled the marsh exiles. His power had been mighty until Lut had defied him. Now the big otter languished.

Harn's eyes closed and, while he napped, Fingertaker reached the river. It droned in the reedbeds; he felt its thrust, a growing force as he weakened. The water pummelled. It took no account of his exhaustion. In every swirl life pulsated, a

113

world of microscopic hustle, of mini-monsters and beauties, and shoals of great tall-finned feeders. The flow cared nothing for his frailty. The old dog fought the current. It was dark where the bank rose, roots of scrub jutting weirdly. Crannies gurgled. Far behind, headlamps stabbed, drawing closer, and he paused in the shadows.

The beams swept the river. As they gleamed, the motor's growl became louder. The road ran by the stream and the sedges were floodlit. Fowl grew restive. Geese hissed in the rushes – 'Beware, the removers!' – and a young moorhen bolted, running long-legged at the floodline. With a roar the van passed, a brief menace, eyes blazing, then sped towards the valley. The otter bobbed in an eddy. Choking fumes hung above him. They drifted off and he struggled up stream towards a sweeter scent – elder.

Smells of former haunts thickened. He rested often. The journey taxed him, but old swims and holts beckoned. The grizzled dog otter gritted. There was a score to be settled. He knew what had to be done and his will was obstinate.

At sun-up the boy watched the nursery from the reeds. Yellow iris was blooming and soon flowering rush would unfurl small pink petals on clustered umbels. He scratched an ear. Gnats were humming. All around, the river's green jungle was at its height, so dense much of the stream flowed invisibly. The youngster straightened. For a moment a breath of wind, opening the reeds to show gliding alleys, ran the reach then was gone. He peered intently at the holt's mouth.

Grinning, he watched the cubs crawl from the darkness. Twice before he had seen them, gazing out for their mother, who would haul them inside when she came back to them. Meantime, they blinked at the river, tiny eyes in snub faces. Its soft prattle pleased them, as did the wing song of insects and the carolling of larks above meadows. Sounds impressed the small otters. Their heads turned to the noises: the drone of bees toiling, the lay of sedge warblers. And now a plop scared the infants. Round faces vanished, to reappear with hesitation.

The water voles and their brood of young were diving. The

chubby male sat in the rushes, alert for danger, which he knew would come quietly, for all his foes moved with stealth, from rat and stoat to the pike and heron. 'Aaeeh!' Through the path of sliding brilliance came the dark-banded giant with the undershot muzzle. As he approached, the beasts saw him. The voles saw Esox. So did Corbie the crow, who was in the sycamore. The boy espied the swift bandit. Only the cubs saw no danger, their eyes filled with sun-stars where the blue sky was mirrored.

'Just stay there,' the boy muttered. 'Don't you go near the water. Not till Bugle is with you.'

He did not think they would venture further since they still walked unsteadily and two, at least, were very timid, quick to duck into the darkness and squeal for their mother. But one, a little pot-bellied dog cub, had a lick of Lut's bravado. At six weeks he was precocious. He had a tottering swagger, a cocksure expression all too much like his father's, and took a step or two now with chirpy nonchalance. Halting, the silky midget collapsed and scratched a pale collar with needle claws. Then wobbled bravely up the strand to the leafy bank. The boy laughed quietly. The tiny otter, flecked with seeds from the grasses, almost smothered by herbage, strutted comically. 'Little Lut!' The lad pondered the likeness. 'Another clown,' he murmured, smiling. 'Another uppity savage! Stay away from the water, you dauntless dwarf!'

Esox swirled. The voles had fled and the boy pitched a stone to drive off the pike, which slunk darkly upriver. The splash startled the cub. His litter mates had gone to earth. He would have followed but the ripples from the stone proved too attractive and, flat nose wrinkling, Lut's son sniffed the current. A slight zephyr, stirring thickets, brought blossom to the water in pale drifting spangles through which the cub's reflection beckoned. Intrigued, the infant leaned forward.

Now the boy looked on anxiously. At last, alarmed for the cub's safety, he abandoned his hideout, wading briskly through the sedges towards the round ball of fur, which recoiled from him. He was stopped by a huff of anger. Wildly, Bugle burst from the water to the riverbank. The bitch was sodden, back spiked with wet guard hairs, her mouth agape. She faced the urchin. In the warm amber light, blebs of spit flew towards him as her warning exploded. Sideways she eyed the cub possessively.

'Come on, Bugle.' The boy held still in the shallows. 'I'd not hurt him. I'm only here to be helpful.'

She hissed, incisors glinting.

'You should know me by now,' pressed the lad, his tone testy, 'Lut's pal, standing watch to protect you. Little Lut was in danger.'

Bubbles rose. With a slosh the surface broke and Lut himself left the current. The adult dog climbed the rock, an eel coiled at his jowls. He surveyed the reach proudly. The eel was young, about a foot long, pale brown, the hue of thickly creamed coffee and glistening with mucus. Lut munched it head first, working greedily tailwards, ignoring the others. The cubs had yet to be weaned and Bugle had eaten. Her gaze remained on the urchin. 'Tell her, Lut,' said the youngster, his jeans soaking up water, 'that I'm not here to harm you. We're old friends of the river. Tell her how we went punting. Tell her that I cared for you. For Pete's sake,' he said, offended, 'she doesn't have to go on so!'

Lut grunted. He licked his chops. The cub was whimpering. Tail stiff, the small creature lurched wonkily towards the bitch, making plaintive squeaks. Once more she spat then, snatching up the wayward infant, slipped swiftly to the tunnel and disappeared. The boy shrugged. 'Females,' he reflected, hands in pockets, 'they can fly off the handle. She'll come round to me.' Lut dived, swimming near him. The cubs were safe for the moment and the lad sloshed down river, spotting trout in rocky shadows. The otter porpoised by the sedges. When they came to the jetty, the animal vanished and the boy left the water under cover of giant hogweed to dry in the sunshine.

In a while the sky clouded. Far away, thunder rumbled, and though the vale would soon brighten, for the time it was sombre. He heard the sound of tyres rasping. The lane was steep to the ferry, twisting and dusty. There was no rain in the clouds, only dry creaky groaning and sultry heat, despite which the boy shivered, crouching low in the weeds as the van hauled into sight, stopping close to them. Tall and blistering, the great plants were luxuriant, bearing buds like portmanteaux. Through the leaves he watched the men ditch their rubbish. Beer cans spewed from the cab, plastic cartons and fag ends.

His flesh had goose-pimpled.

He heard words, grunted comments; smelled cigarettes burning. A belch. The fat man spoke: 'Time I had me an otter.' Then, 'Keep your mind on the big stuff,' came from his slight, trap-faced partner.

'The place is stiff with it.'

A laugh.

'And unkeepered!'

The van was still filthy. Scared to move, the boy listened. A cassette released a pop tune – then perhaps they were snoozing, for the cab became silent, and he tried to ease backwards. But a huge hogweed stopped him, the whole green bag of tricks shaking until he feared the men must spot him, and he trembled himself. His marsh memories were vivid – of their cargo, their weapons. He had a nightmare: he was shut in with their victims, thrown in the back with the carnage, the meat and blood, fur and feathers, and the fat man was saying, 'I told you I'd have one, I'd get me an otter!'

In the weeds, the boy listened. The woods had grown noisy, a bedlam of voices. The van had upset the morning, especially the rooks who, sensing violence, flew in great dusky circles, protests clamorous.

'We'll need more ammo.' The cab talk resumed.

'And carriers – to help with the humping.'

'No problem. There'll be no problems, just two old bats, one at the Hall, one at the cottage. A brace of geriatrics.' The driver started the motor. With a lurch the van reversed, turning tightly at the jetty, flushing birds from the hedges as it snarled up the gradient. It took the rooks an hour to settle. The boy did not wait one minute. Elbows flying, he crashed through hogweed and burdock, leaped the boatman's fence headlong and ran, bawling, up the path. To lie low no longer mattered. Lying low would not stop the removers.

'They'll kill the otters!' he shouted. 'And Hunter's deer! They've got guns! They'll come shooting and destroying! There'll be a massacre!'

117

A long heat had descended. All day the sun scorched the cornfields and at night moths teemed restlessly. It was lizard weather, the kind of spell when the kestrel toils to hover, when the smell of tar hangs in lanes, and tractors head berserker dust storms on thirsting slopes. Pools grew shallow. On the millpond a matt film of algae surrounded bloated white lilies while scores of watersnails surfaced. Towards Hill Farm the dyke hummed like the tropics.

Prowling its bilges, Lut found dragonflies hawking, thin wings crackling. The heat hammered down. He dragged through warm water. It was time to siesta, lie up in the shadows, but Lut was vigilant. He had seen duck in hasty flight and heard snipe utter warnings. 'Fingertaker! Beware, the old one!' He lurched by lank yellow hawkweed. Its wilting heads dangled. Soon he came to the culvert where he had hidden from the farm dogs, and now, reaching its far end, looked out on the hillside. Foxglove drooped in the hedges. He saw his old foes. They were with the farm stockman, slowly driving cows homewards, but the dogs were moving tiredly.

Lut went back by the haybarn. He saw no sign of Fingertaker. The white owls would be resting, awaiting dusk before ghosting where the tang of dung wafted and the 'snoring' of owlets proclaimed hungry gullets. By night the meadow-sweet shone there with a strange lunar pallor which recalled the crests of sea waves. Lut remembered the breakers bombarding the marsh wall, the chill shock as he strove through them. He returned to the river. Unlike the sea, it was tepid.

He swirled down the stream, grunting. Horseflies clustered in meadows. The otter swam heavily, diving from insects. Their drone was mournful. He missed the bright chirp of nestlings, suppressed in airless thickets. He missed the mud slides, hard-baked now and cracking. Lut rolled limply in the water. Tornadoing swifts mocked him, screaming over the surface. They made their own cooling airstreams and he paddled with envy, annoyed by the warning.

Fingertaker!

The cat lay on the jetty. Had the cat seen the old one? She spat, sharing no secrets and he cursed, faring onwards. Nothing moved in the reedbeds. Rank and hazy, the banks steamed, deep in plantains and nettles. The reach was breathless. A damp finger, held aloft, would have detected no motion in the heat which blanched the duckweed and reddened the dock seeds. A squirrel slouched in the herbage. Loping lazily, it sprang to a tree bole, execrating the amphibian. 'Tch-ch-ch!'

Lut swore back without stopping.

Black Corbie was feeding. In the grass by the river a partridge had nested. A dozen buff eggs had sat there until the gulls cracked them open, gorged and left the shells scattered. Some of the cups still held food and the crow dipped and guzzled. 'Fingertaker?' Corbie leered, gulping egg yolk. The 'third bird' did not miss much, for while his paired neighbours brooded the bachelor scouted. 'Just take care,' croaked the corvid. He threw back his head and swallowed. 'Take your nose to the wharf, Lut.'

'Fingertaker?'

'The old one has been there.'

Lut swam on, his rage mounting.

Ewes, clipped white, lay in thorn shade. A bunting piped out its sun-song. Lut would kill the giant this time. The old

119

one would perish. The bunting's trill turned to indolence. Lut had proved his ascendancy. He savoured the memory. He had fought with inspiration: the ruse, the stab, the bold action! Blood had flowed. Mud had swirled as they sank in the marsh brook, the river weed closing, and he had clung like a limpet. Fingertaker had weakened. Now Lut was the master – Lut who routed the rat pack, who landed the sea eel. By what right was he challenged? Yet he smelled Fingertaker.

As he reached the brick bulwarks he could taste the sharp odour, and climbed the wharf swiftly, leaving puddles on its lichens. Grass pushed up through the bricks. Old mooring rings rusted. He searched warily. There was no doubt of the intrusion. Fingertaker had sprainted and the mark was fresh. But the beast had not lingered. Lut probed bothy and brambles, explored bent grass and swan's lair. The intruder had slipped him. He growled savagely. Suppose the other had flanked him, made straight for the holt? He might now be with Bugle. Lut hit the stream, snarling.

Turning into the flow, he stroked powerfully. The scene was little changed as he headed home. The crow still supped. The otter sped like a tempest. Swifts banked darkly above him. Again, the grey squirrel ranted. Lut hardly noticed. He passed the ferry underwater, cleaving streaming weed gardens. Then, where the woods cast their shadows, he swirled up to throw his whistle of contact through the screened light to Bugle. He heard her answering voice and its note spurred his urgency.

The bitch swam out from the strand, nosed the male and turned back. She was distressed. Lut thrust past her to the tunnel. It was cool in the earth, and he crawled through the tree roots to the nursery chamber. Loud squeaks greeted him. Two wriggling infants ran forward. Lut searched the gloom for the third. Trickling water, he looked into the corners. There was no third cub. One small otter was missing. It was Little Lut.

The clatter echoed. It seemed to fill the wood's vault, then the pigeon had gone, leaving the otter cub blinking, and calm returned. The little animal pondered. While the bitch had searched the river, he had entered the covert, ignoring her call note. The green pavilion had thrilled him. Everywhere, marvels beckoned. He saw snakes and bright beetles. Deer plucked leaves in sunny glades. He had watched rabbits sloppet, and disturbed the woodpigeon, to learn how noisy that bird was when moving through branches.

Now, as stillness resettled, the massive oaks awed him. His mother's voice had grown distant. At last it died altogether, screened by canopied columns, and the cub's boldness wavered. The leafy gloom was unnerving. On a path, the corpse of a shrew had blood on its snout and smelled malodorous. Who knew what had killed it? Whatever *had*, had scorned to eat the scented victim and might still be hungry. The otter cub missed his mother. He liked her voice, her warm tongue when she washed him. But Lut's son was independent and did not bawl for her.

Instead, he crept forward. To keep up spirit, he growled at shadows. Once he scattered young pheasants – their fear of him was consoling – and he chased them ineptly until he fell over. For a while he lay breathless, then raised a small head and snuffled, his nose in querulous wrinkles. He smelled water. Few smells were more familiar. On shaky legs he advanced, barging boldly through thickets. Briars and bindweed ensnared him, catching hold as he lolloped. White coronels nodded. He could hear the cascade now, but it was hardly a river and he paused, disappointed. A small brook was tumbling from the mossy embrasure to wind away through the ground-growth. The midget followed it.

Cub-sized, the woodland rill pottered along. While it trickled, he paddled, enjoying the dampness, to hop out as it deepened and drew close to the main stream. Demoiselle flies were dancing. A wagtail watched, its rump jerking. The bobbing bird eyed the confluence, saw the otter cub halt there, scratch and sniff where the stream lapped. Saw, too, the pike leave the weedbed and slide to the bank's rim. The wagtail fluttered. Esox bent his gaze upwards. The cub was wobbling. 'Teeter over,' the pike muttered. 'Few will miss you, small otter. The bitch was warned. Since she spawned on the pike swim, I'll take my toll.'

His rayed fins flickered. Anglers yarned about Esox: told

how he snatched trout from fishhooks, dragged waterfowl under and, according to the boatman, had attacked bulging keepnets. Hunger kept him ferocious. He needed food in big quantities and so far had found it, for he had yet to grow lank, or his immense head ungainly. He was huge but still swift, at the height of his havoc. He could also be patient and now Esox lay quietly beneath the bank. He had a grudge against otters and waited greedily.

Tired, the cub rested. The sun scorched. Heaving by, the stream puzzled the infant, at once a friend and a stranger, the home landmarks missing. There was no rock; no shady sycamore to cool him. The heat pounded. There was no strand. This bemused the small otter, who longed for the tunnel, the moist earth of the holt. He snapped at a blue fly. Far off, the bitch whistled. The sound, skirling where the stream curved, reached him faintly across the current and his eyes gleamed. With a squeak, he nosed the water. Its volume was daunting. The cub had watched Bugle swimming, seen Lut in the river, but never gone with them. The young were left on the bank when the bitch fished. He dithered.

Again the whistle came thinly. It seemed to call from the far bank, a shrill, anxious summons. The cub was balked by the water. He fretted. Twice he braced himself to plunge; twice he funked the current. Little Lut seldom wavered, and he snarled at his reflection with mounting annoyance. At last, shutting his eyes, he simply stepped into space. When he took stock, he was floating, the pike three lengths from him. He saw the decked teeth approaching, then was shoved rudely backwards. A strange beast had joined them, a great sickly old otter, more dead than living, yet awesome.

Fingertaker's growl trembled.

It said, 'The cub is mine, Esox. Touch the cub and I'll slay you, for the cub is of my tribe and I am the Marsh Lord.' The grizzled jaws twisted. Clan was clan, thought the old one. He had come for Lut, for revenge, but would not see the cub harmed. 'Look and fear me, marauder. I am Lord of the Survivors and the pike will respect me.' He winced, the ache in him stabbing. 'Kick!' he ordered the young one. 'Kick your legs; reach the sedges!'

122

Esox circled, frustrated. But the pike was voracious, his cold eye determined. The old otter was feeble and the river shark hovered. Fingertaker was dying. The pike's chill gaze shifted. The cub floundered, paws dabbling, and the predator wheeled, slewing out around the veteran. A raking tube, the fish glinted. Little Lut paddled vainly. Instinct kept the cub swimming but the strong current nudged, pushed him farther from safety. Fingertaker lurched grimly. Slowly, his racked body manoeuvred to screen the cub.

Again, the pike sought an opening. With a lash, he swam downstream, hauled beam-on to the current and waited, tail switching. The small otter was spinning. He tried to hold his stern steady but the flow was too powerful. Like a twig he was borne on, fur slicked by its drenching, ever closer to Esox. The old dog otter wallowed, yet a spark remained in him. 'Kick, small one; keep kicking!' And as the pike charged, snout looming, some last reserve in Fingertaker drove him savagely.

The river dazzled. There was a high, unyielding glare to the valley which the coiling stream mirrored while the cub watched in terror. Socking waves ringed the surface. At their centre the fight raged, fish and beast turning turtle, rayed fins and spiked guard hairs, flared operculum, whiskers. The sun struck their flexed bodies. A banded flank glittered. Spray trailed from webbed forefeet. Then the toilers were diving, leaving froth in angry bubbles, and the cub saw them dimly, raising sand from the bottom as they whirled, locked together.

Drifting, he whistled for Bugle, a wild squeak of panic. His small legs were heavy. The duellists had vanished. All he could see was sand darkening the water so that a dense pall swirled downstream, flecked with shimmering fish scales. Scarcely breathing, he waited. In a moment the flood boiled and a huge tailfin lashed him. Spuming, the tail sank and, as it did, the pike tore free from the old one to limp beaten upriver.

Fingertaker towered slowly. There was an odd fever in him. Almost sightless, his eyes blazed. Shades of old conflicts filled him, of marsh wars and victories; marsh storms drummed out his triumphs. His mouth wrenched suddenly.

The drifting cub whimpered. Weakly, he cried again but the veteran ignored him, sliding down through the wavelets to the shadowy weedbeds, no longer in torment.

Lut's son floated on. The stream bent and slithered, hedged by mallow and reed mace. By and by, the sky glowered, and warm unwavering rain fell before the glare regained mastery. The cub had given up squealing. His mouth was shut to the water, a spinning head dizzy. Yet pictures flicked in it: now of slopes, now of trees, of a plateau-shaped boulder. Otter Rock! He resumed his shrill 'Mayday'. A minute later Bugle snatched him from the current. He was soused, but as alive as Fingertaker was dead when the evening cooled.

The hand which grabbed him was coarse-veined. It joined a
walnut-coloured arm from which the tattoo of a water serpent glared balefully. Squirming, the boy yelped, 'Let go –
heck, you're hurting!' then, with hastening passion, 'You've
got to do something. They'll kill the otters. Not just the
otters, the deer and birds. They don't care; they kill
anything.'

'Inside! We'll talk in the cottage.'

'Let go, I've done nothing!'

Indoors, the boatman said, 'Bide still and listen. You're in
trouble. You're in trouble with Hunter. If he finds you, he'll
skin you. Same with her from the Welfare. You lied again,
you young beggar. Still running loose! Pledged reform and
still on the river! It's me they come to for answers. Have I
seen you? Where are you?'

'The fat man's going to kill them.'

'Never mind the tall stories, we've heard too many.'

'I only lied for the otters. You've got to help. The men will
murder them, kill the cubs. Three cubs,' he chanted with
fervour, 'but the fat man will have them.'

'You don't give up.'

'It's true.'

The man sighed. He lit his pipe, its scent filling the small parlour. A few sticks of plain furniture stood in corners, the cat on the best chair. There was a box on a table. The box was rich in patina, a piece on its own, wrought with care by the boatman through some forgotten winter. It was of wood worked in marquetry. On the lid was a schooner, fully rigged, the sea veneered like green satin while, around the escutcheon, a flaring sun formed a compass, each golden point lettered. The boatman said, 'Otters! Beasts are beasts, boy – not family. They take their chances.'

'They need protecting.'

The man squinted at the box. He could not have made it these days. His sight was going and his hands had grown tremulous. He said, 'It's the *truth* needs protecting, for ye've the tongue of a magician.'

'I heard them!' The boy swung on him fiercely. 'They came down the lane there. She saw them, the cat. She could tell you. And the rooks could; those old birds can smell danger. They've still not settled.'

'And that's it?'

'It's all true. I was sat in the hogweed. They've got guns. I saw them first on the marshes and now they're here – the removers!'

The boatman eyed the boy sternly. He had seen the van turning. No one in those parts was moving, and Hunter's deer were wide open. The man wondered. Venison fetched high prices. He turfed the cat from the armchair. 'Sit down, lad.' Pipe smoke swirled in blue eddies. 'The lane's a free byway. There's no law against parking. Folk can lose their direction or just stop to rest there.'

'Killers! They fill their van,' the urchin answered. 'Meat or pelt, they kill for it. Deer or otter. They'll be back. . . .' He broke off, his mind arid. 'I won't let them,' he shouted. 'I'll prevent them. I've got to.'

The man stroked the schooner. His fingers were rough, but their tips caressed the woodwork. Behind the ship was a lighthouse, a thin veneer of low coastline. He had slipped in a flagpole, the finest of slivers. 'You remind me,' he grunted; 'you take me back, you young truant.' He opened the box,

126

seeking out the old picture. It was foxed now and faded, the photo of a youngster. He said, 'That's the fellow. Ran away to sea, that one. Wild as a polecat; full o' stories, romances. You remind me, young beggar; take me back to the old times.'

'Is it *you*?'

'You'd not think so.' He closed the lid on remembrance. 'That's art,' the man boasted quickly, 'a box fit for treasures. There's veneers of all shades there: amber, honey and red-wood. See how the grain's been used for sea swell? That's artistry. That's the work of a craftsman. You make a box like that one day and you can be proud, lad. It's fit for Hunter's place – that is, the Hall in its heyday. Hunter's Hall when it was shipshape.'

'Hunter's deer will be murdered!'

The boatman cocked a thick eyebrow. 'Guns, you say? You saw guns, boy?'

'Shotguns, rifles.'

'If you're having me on. . . .'

'Guns, I swear!'

'Maybe we ought to warn Hunter, not that the beggar deserves it. You know he'll tear the ears off you? That's your business. If I go, you come with me, and you'd better convince him. All I saw was a van.'

They went up by the river and through the woods. Doves were growling, the dim arcade slashed with sunbeams towards the Hall. Tangled brakes of thorn bristled. Doubly dark beneath the oak dome, they played tricks on the vision, forging weird shapes with shadows. 'Look!' the boy whispered, halting. A bulky form crossed the footpath. The fat man was not armed but, where his jacket was open, a marksman's belt glinted. The pillared gloom cloaked him. 'You saw that!' the boy blurted.

'I'm not blind,' said the boatman. Their pace increased.

Bugle lay on the rock. Shoals were present and she studied their movements. The stream was provident. Richly stocked, it had extended her knowledge of fish and fishing. She had met the grayling and learned its rise-action, which seldom changed. Midge or mayfly, the grayling rose to insects with snapping force, making a mound on the water, and broken ripples. The trout rose slowly and sucked in his victim. His surface sign was a dimple, then rings spreading smoothly. Both fish were swift. Bugle liked slower swimmers, caught with less time and trouble, for the cubs sapped her energy.

Now dace and roach swam together. The two species often mingled, and this shoal was substantial. Scores of fish lazed beneath her. The size of many was decent, but one was outstanding, a big roach, the leader. Fish leaders had this quality, always dwarfing their followers. None of the others was half the size of its commander and the otter's gaze fixed him. He was the fish to outwit or he would bolt in an instant, the whole shoal behind him.

She yawned. The bitch was not hurried. Until she moved, the fish would browse, and the warm rock was soothing. She could observe the holt from it while she was at rest from the nursery. The brood's demands increased daily, the three almost weaned. They were tiring. She cleaned her toes, nibbling briskly on skin then licking the hair flat. Next, full length, she pressed her throat to the boulder, eyes still on the water. Small fish squirmed to the surface. Drifting scraps of weed drew them. But the big roach was watchful, his minions around him, and did not move.

Three specks hauled from the sky wall. Widely spaced, they came nearer, heron cries ringing. Over Potman's they slewed, lost perhaps fifty feet, and flew up the valley at twice that height. At Hill Farm, Harn jinked heavily. The young birds with him circled. Drifting widely around the oak wood, they tailed their flightmaster's landing, a long glide to the river, to stall and pitch to the sedges. The fledglings cranked their necks, wide-eyed. The vale was new to them. Strutting, they flipped black crests barely free of their chick-down, and sparred for positions. They were slimmer and paler than the older bird.

Bugle cursed them. As their sails skimmed the reach, the fish leader had darted, disappearing up river. In a flash, his finned army had followed. The otter glared at the herons. The young were jousting, jumping up from the bank, wings flapping, beaks crossed in mock combat. Harn barked and they fell quietly to fishing, heads drawn into their shoulders. From time to time they called hoarsely, passing on the stream's gossip.

'Fingertaker is dead.'

'The Marsh Lord routed Esox.'

'Saved the cub.'

'Then was gone.'

Shadows lengthened. It was still warm and aged lanes, like old war trenches, slumbered, their brambles dense with green bullets. 'Lut rules,' said the herons, 'and Bugle's cubs prosper.'

'Almost weaned.'

'Will soon swim.'

'In the stream which is once more an otter stream!'

'Huh!' the old bird objected. 'Three cubs and two adults?' He croaked derisively. 'An otter *reach*,' Harn corrected. They had much to discover. 'A *heron* stream!'

Lut joined Bugle soon after. Her reserved mood was over and they lounged close together, sometimes licking each other. At last, taking to water, they made a search for the lost shoal. It must have moved a great distance. Giving up, they turned back, Lut exploring the margins. Dipping rays struck the sedges. In the brazen pre-gloaming, tilting banks held the heat and green frogs basked along them. Lut shuffled the incline. A frog jumped. It sprang from under his nose, towering clear across the sedges to splash in the water. The second leaped with time to spare, almost landing on Bugle, who swam near the shallows.

She required little prompting. While her mate drove the herbage, she kept pace with him offshore, prepared for the divers. At each plop, she ducked under, twisting after the quarry as its long thighs propelled it, her armed forepaws stabbing. Lut was rorty as a piglet. Cavorting, he charged the bank hump-backed, elated as the frogs soared. Harn had flown with his offspring. Harn did not fear the otters – something else had alarmed him. But the beasts were too busy, too frenzied to notice, and when finally they rested the stream seemed deserted. Bugle gathered her harvest. Frogs dangling, she made for home.

Lut paused briefly. Eels lurked on that stretch and he

turned some stones before leaving. Out of luck, he swam quickly, overtaking the bitch to gain the rock and wait for her. The river crooned. Near the bend its song varied, a high whirr in the harmony. Lut slipped into the rushes. He knew the reel's languid descant as the line crossed the water, and spotted the angler. Hunter sported tall waders. Reeling in, he moved up by the far bank, each stiff-legged step gurgling. He was gaunt as a heron. Around his hatband were trout flies.

Inshore, the stream was fickle. Where sand had lodged, the man's shins were just covered. Elsewhere, holes plunged him deeper and he leaned on the current, mumbling oaths through tight lips. Swooping branches engulfed him. Some he ducked, some he detoured. For a while he was hidden in a cave pool of foliage, emerging near the rock where the sycamore straggled. Its keys touched his shoulders. 'Ah!' He stopped by the strand, catching sight of the tunnel. With a grunt, he bent slightly, scanning the tracks there. 'Damned cosy,' he muttered. 'Full house, shouldn't wonder.'

He held still and a hush fell. Only the flow could be heard – and a plop in the reeds. The bitch had dropped a dead frog. Hunter whirled, facing Lut and their eyes clashed. Neither blinked. 'You can stare,' the man grumbled. 'Damn your snout, don't *you* blame me. Don't echo the brat's tune; I've heard the reproaches. I'll not harm you. Things have changed. Every damned thing is changing. They'll do their worst when I'm gone, when the vandals take over. But you're welcome till then, beast.'

Hunter glared at the heavens. Angry clouds were encroaching, riding in on the evening. Storms were threatening. The otter dived. The old hunting man grunted. Alone where the weed trailed, he flicked his rod and the casting reel whistled. Gnats hung over him.

Part Three

Otter Reach

Hunter scowled. 'He was right to inform us. The boy did right and we need him. He knows these damned ruffians.'

'How things have changed!' cried the boatman.

'Times have changed. We must mobilize.'

'What you mean,' said the boatman, 'is that you're going to give orders. You'll be content then, you crackpot.'

'I mean I'll not see my deer shot. We need a plan of defence, not your fool remarks.'

The boy's gaze wandered. They held council at the Hall, the two old men and the urchin, around a great table. Tarnished armour stood guard, the walls encrusted with weapons, swords and shields in fierce clusters. The blackened fireplace was monstrous. A battle steed might have stood there and tossed its head freely. Dwarfed, the youngster sat forward. A vast chair towered behind him, its back a carved rampart. High above, a bird fluttered, as in the halls of the Saxons, at home in the rafters. He said, 'The men are recruiting?'

'They'll come mob-handed,' said the boatman.

'Confound the louts,' Hunter ranted, 'I'll teach them!' He

stood up, swaying slightly. 'They need rough handling. Let the louts come, I'll baste 'em!'

'Armed men?'

'Armed!' Hunter lurched to the wall. 'Damn their arms.' He snatched a sabre and twirled it, mesmerizing the youngster. 'We've stood armed here through history. Let 'em come with their arms, man!' The boy was gripped by the image, the haggard figure, its patched jacket flying. He could almost have liked Hunter. As a scourge of the removers, sword in hand, the man assumed new dimensions. His sunken orbs blazed for justice. If only he were younger. He seemed too old for a champion – despite his fire, a frail match for the fat man.

'He's mad,' the boatman snapped bluntly. 'We're not dealing with striplings.'

'Rabble!' Hunter said hoarsely.

'Armed villains.'

'Louts! You think we can't rout them?'

The boy considered the boatman. His tattooed arms were folded, eyes raised in exasperation to where cobwebs stretched from helmets to soaring beams. The boy shared his misgivings. The lad knew the removers, had seen their armoury. He recalled the guns in the cab, the bandoliers and the bullets. Yet his heart was with Hunter, for someone had to do something. Someone had to take action. 'I'll help.' He thrust a hand up, fist rounded. 'I'll help you to stop them.'

'Bah!' The boatman rose stiffly. 'The local bobby can sort 'em; he's paid for it.'

'He lives miles off. He can't sit here nights, waiting.'

'Damn right, boy.' Hunter's glance was approving. 'Young fellow's got the makings. We'll man our own lines, by thunder! We'll fight our corner!'

'*We?*' the boatman said drily.

'We'll post guards, lie in ambush.'

'*You*, mister. Me and the boy won't be joining, not for this war.'

The urchin watched Hunter's face flush. The man seemed to shudder, the sword dropping so its point bit the floor and it stood upright, twitching. The chased handguard trembled. At length it stopped and the man's cheeks had emptied. Still speechless, Hunter spluttered. In the end, he found phrases.

134

'Sit down,' he choked. 'I'll ignore that. I'll not tolerate dodgers. Each man does his duty in this campaign.'

The boy jumped up. 'I'll keep lookout.'

'You take care,' said the boatman. 'You're too quick into trouble.'

Hunter said, 'He's got spirit.'

'Changed your tune, you blamed firebrand.'

'He's willing.'

'I'll watch the river,' the boy said. 'If they advance from the bottoms, I'll pass the word. I know the tracks where the stream flows.' He thought of Hunter's locked boathouse, the prize there. She was spanking, a seagull. 'With the dinghy,' he wheedled, 'I could scout a lot farther, patrol the whole woodside.' Sail with Lut and the otters! 'I could handle her.'

'Like the punt,' growled the boatman. 'Who'll rescue you next time?'

Hunter said, 'He's keen, dammit.' The scowl had lifted. 'If I launch her, I'll take him. I'll watch the young wrecker. Are we ready for stations?' He stomped briskly to his gun rack and said, selecting a brace of twelve-bores, 'Let's get the tools issued.' He tossed a gun to the boatman. 'Try it, man. Does it suit you? Is the weight right? I've a thirteen – take your pick. Choose your shot. I'd say fives should bestir them. There's a boxful. . . .'

'You're off your head, Hunter!'

'We'll teach 'em!'

'I'm not taking your shotgun.' It was shoved on the table and the boy smelled the gun oil. 'You mad dotard,' wheezed the boatman, 'I'm not shooting at people. If you think that, you're crazy. You'll hurt someone. You'll kill someone, you crackpot. I'll do turns keeping lookout, but not with that weapon. Any trouble, I'm ducking – you get on with it.' He jerked a thumb at the urchin. 'And forget the lad, mister. I'll take care of the young 'un.'

'He'll be with me.'

'With *me*, ye blamed tyrant!'

'Who's commanding, you blackguard?'

The cry skirled on the river. It was a call from prehistory, the otter's call. The boy listened. The sky had coloured.

135

Salmon-pink above the levels, it blazed red where the sun sank – and he moved from the jetty. Owl sounds wound through the vale softly, the low tremblings of summer; dogs yapped in the distance. On plimsolled feet he passed the PRIVATE – KEEP OUT board, padding silently. Prints of heron stitched the margins. He saw the seals of the marsh bitch. Above the woods, the Hall's chimneys were darkening as he reached his post.

From the boathouse he viewed the river. A moorhen clucked in the reedbed. Between fronds, her tail signalled, its twitch anxious as her black infants followed. The tiny golliwogs zigzagged. Sensing danger, they vanished – now dotting the surface; next instant underwater, where they streamed towards cover, bobbing up near their parent. Something moiled through the sedges. There was a slosh; a head glinted. 'Lut?' The boy probed the gloaming. 'It's me, I'm on watch, Lut.'

A lone duck speared south, squawking. The otter lofted his neck; shedding water, it shimmered, aglow in the sky-blaze. A look of greed crossed Lut's features, the expectation of tidbits, but the boy produced nothing.

'Keep alert,' he said sternly. 'They'll have guns when they come, Lut, and traps. Unless we're sharp they'll surprise us.' And drench the vale with their carnage. Only Hunter could stop them, the old man with nine fingers – the old destroyer of otters. 'We have to trust him,' the boy said. 'No one else, Lut, can stop them.'

Lut grew bored, his hopes dwindling. Talk held no fascination and the animal yawned, still with a half chance of cadging but increasingly restive. If the boy proved unfruitful, Lut would move to the frog banks or maybe troll for crayfish. He dived and rose, treading water. He knew the lairs of the crayfish and where eels hid by daylight. He had been reared on that reach, knew its depths like his forepaws.

'If you see them, lie low, Lut. Keep the cubs under cover. See that Bugle's in hiding.'

The otter rolled with the current. Tired of jibberish, he submerged. The boy waited. He heard a door at the Hall slam. Birds were pitching to roost, thickets rustling. Beyond the hill, a vixen yelped: a single high-pitched aspiration, like the whoop of an asthmatic. A hare appeared. As hares will, she missed the figure in the foreground, her attention at greater distance, and the lad could have touched her. Neither boy nor beast shifted. Then, pulling in her long hind legs, the doe sat up, mauve eyes bulging. Still, she missed the crouched youngster, stirred at last by a sound to dash off through the herbage, her black-tipped ears flattened.

Hunter limped from the covert.

'You're punctual, boy,' he said gruffly. He paused, eyeing the cloud grid. The night would be dark. Pintail whirled in the sunset, and a scrawny fist squeezed the shotgun, but it stayed at his armpit. 'Let's get the craft floated.' The man opened the boathouse. Varnish gleamed. The dinghy was pristine, barely touched by the water. Slack-jawed, the boy surveyed her. 'Push, young fellow.' They ran her out and, as she dipped to the river, the lad recalled another launching, his fight with the old vessel. This was how it should happen. Wavelets kissed the bright planking. They were almost deferential.

'Jump aboard.' Hunter stowed the gun for'ard. Taking the oars, he said, 'Sit at the stern, boy. Be still. Keep your eyes skinned.'

'Are we patrolling up river?'

'You'll find out. Less chat, blast it.'

The boy buttoned his sleeves. The air had cooled; insects were biting. Drained, the eastern sky glimmered, no longer red but corn-coloured, the last throw of daylight. It bathed the crowns of the oak wood and lit the pale rind of birch poles. It washed bluffs drilled by martins. Here and there it touched pylons and, where old meadows languished, gilded time-rotted fences whose pales marched like lemmings down banks to drown. The dome blackened. Hunter groaned as his spine curved. He sculled smoothly but slowly, each stroke drawing grumbles. But the boat did not protest. The little craft whispered sweetly, shafting ripples at withies, teasing banks as she passed them, her wash a mere flutter.

'She's a spanker,' the boy breathed. 'She's a bird, that's a fact, sir. Not a leak in her, nowhere!'

'Never mind the damned dinghy. You're on watch – keep a look out!'

'Will they come about this time?'

'Dusk will suit 'em.'

'Sneak up in the shadows.' He felt safe on the river; strangely safe with the oarsman. 'But they can't hide the van,' he said, scanning the ridges, 'That's the thing to watch out for.' He combed the deep-shaded hedgerows. Bats were winging, changing guard with the swallows, and a low mist was thickening. It swirled apart as the boat forayed, closing quickly behind her, muffling the sounds of oars and rowlocks. The boy thought of the fat man and his ferret-faced partner; of the chase in the snow, their howls ringing. Misty shapes moved in fields. They were cattle, he hoped.

Then the woods closed in densely. Abruptly, the light dimmed and the man said, 'What's that?' with a brusqueness that startled.

'Otter Rock.' The boy regarded him sharply.

'Young eyes. Wish I had 'em.'

'You still fish.'

'In hope, young fellow.'

The urchin looked at the shotgun. 'And shoot?' he asked, the doubt nagging.

'Raise a poacher, I'll bag him!' Hunter's growl reassured. He was convincingly fearsome. 'Blast it, boy, I'm not senile. I'm not your friend from the ferry. You show me the beggars!'

He rowed in silence, merely grunting. Loamy smells filled the chasm, and a sound like leaves rustling. Yet the air remained heavy, the noise eerily persistent, getting louder. Trees thinned and the mill loomed. Ahead, its gushing now thunderous, the weir shone in the half-light, a smooth downpour from the crumbling stone sill. Hunter rested. The boy watched the stream tumble. Untiring, it deluged, at the lip thickly sheeted then smashed by rocks into wild, fizzing rapids. These frothed into the catch pool, a deep mist-veiled basin strewn with bricks from the mill, and fallen masonry.

The place was daunting, the naked flow awesome. The boy held tight as they drifted, rocking now in the turbulence between two moods of water, its peace and swift violence. A skull rose and dipped suddenly. Hunter's back was turned to it but the boy glimpsed the otter. When Lut's bubble trail faded, he said, 'All clear up to this point. No enemies sighted.'

'Early days,' Hunter answered.

'Would you like me to row?'

'Damn it, stick to your post, man.'

They turned downstream in silence, the mist grey around them. Hunter's face was in shadow. At the stern the boy brooded. He would like to trust the old oarsman, get to know the man better, but belief was not easy. He said at length, 'What you reckoned, about the otter crash happening – was it true? Were they poisoned? Was it stuff like you told me, or did you invent that?'

'Invent?' The word echoed. 'B'God, invention's your talent! Pesticide doomed the otters; polluted streams, poisoned fish. They banned the muck, but too late, child. Hunting wasn't the reason. Perhaps it didn't help, either, but it wasn't the main cause.'

'You'd not molest otters now?'

'No. I've told you once, damn you. Nor if I had my time over. Just damned deer-poaching cowboys and insolent urchins.'

'We *will* stop them, won't we?'

'Damn-fool questions!' The veteran's voice wavered. Awkwardly, he took off his jacket and thrust it at the youngster. 'Night's cool, put it round you. Skin your eyes and keep quiet. Blasted questions – you confuse me.'

Lut lay up by the footpath. The track was a jungle, summer's growth at its most copious. Densely tangled, it left the bank inaccessible except from the river – an undisturbed garden. At its bottom grew horsemint, forget-me-nots, crowfoot. Bines of bryony gleamed, overhanging the reed wall. Red valerian billowed. Every yard of verge bristled; the riverside was sumptuous.

Amid this feast, almost smothered by verdure, a small creek formed a mirror, full of blue-green reflections, aside from the torrent. Here the cubs liked to gambol, and now, all in the water, they were encouraged by Bugle. For a while her mate watched them. Their sport was not gentle. They brawled like young furies, shaking, biting each other, their thickset tails thumping.

The rowdy nonsense amused Lut. Ears flat, he gave a broad yawning grin as they dashed from the shallows, tore at plants in their devilment, snatched pebbles. Back in the water, they tussled. The bitch had dived in the main stream. Above the reeds, tops of turbulent clouds rose, the front some way off yet, while a warbler churred fretfully. Bugle brought up a trout. When she had opened the shoulder, the cubs

140

gorged. They ate savagely, snarling, tearing until only the tail was left.

This, the small dog abducted. Growling jealously, he held the remnant with his forefeet and chewed it. The other two sucked their paws, content to rest for the moment. But they were soon up and squabbling. Lut stretched, his eyes wicked. He left their rearing to Bugle but would play when in the spirit – when the old clown came on him – and now he swept past them, buffooning. With a splash he struck the water, bellyflopping to spray them. Unprepared, they drew back; then, with squeals of bravado, charged forward to chase him.

Lut led them in circles. At first, breasting smoothly, they tripped the quiet creek line astern, webbed feet paddling. Soon, he quickened the tempo. Now his whole frame was thrusting, legs tucked up, and he porpoised. Half in fear, the cubs followed. Their apprehension was fleeting. Before long they were whirling, undulating like veterans, describing rings as the pool churned. Lut rollicked, tail whipping. In glee the cubs strove to catch him, outpaced until he slackened, inviting their mauling, which he met with mock outrage.

Bugle towered up in the current. From that street of speeding light she could see the reeds flinching as the wind reached the valley. She did not like its bluster. Scent and sound fled before it, no longer trustworthy warnings. The time had come to move homeward, and she called the cubs.

They were juggling the fishtail. Lut drove them towards her, diving shallowly to rise near the female. The young otters moved slowly. Loath to leave, they stopped to play on the way as the gusts surged. Bugle's voice shrilled. The gale was charging now, roaring, and the stream crankled suddenly. Overriding the flow, waves jogged in drear armies, the sedge-song in dirge, a whining edge to it. Wands of willow were lashing. It was dangerous. Where the black plumes of reeds blew, unexplained evils wafted and Lut, looking at Bugle, sensed the fear in her.

He growled, urging the cubs on. They had their own pace. Swell was slapping the banks, whisking froth in the crannies. The stuff was ochreous, a clay-tinted scum, and two small

141

otters were making the foam fly. Lut pushed them towards Bugle. He looked for the third cub. The dense growth was in turmoil, tossed and splayed as the gale struck, revealing dark places, the raw depths of reed beds. Across the creek a rift opened and Lut saw his namesake. There was no mistaking the cub's waddle. Then the swirling gap closed and the little male vanished.

Quickly, Lut traversed the shallows. Snarled clouds scudded above. Their darkening shapes rampaged, leaping reed walls like demons. He hesitated. Fronds were bending, high pennons wind-torn, and from somewhere in the ferment Lut felt the presence of disaster. He went on, his neck bristling. A barricade of stems shivered. He paused again. Bugle's eyes had unnerved him with their prescience. Again, he went forward, plunging into the bank growth, barging through swaying gardens, his dread mounting.

Little Lut sprawled there grotesquely. He lay where grass had been flattened, trampled down with crude violence, and his head had been shattered. His back was broken. He lay limply, still dripping, a small heap of damp velvet, bemusing the adult. Lut nudged the pathetic shape. No time ago it had been romping, a spry bag of mischief. Now Lut shrank from it, anguished. Distressed, he inched backwards, gaze fixed on the horror. Reedheads streamed in the gale. They were funereal.

Running, Lut reached the river. Abomination prowled the tempest, stalked unseen where fronds quivered, and Bugle would be waiting, two more cubs in danger. He crossed the creek in search of them. Nearby, a vole dived. Waves loomed angrily. Spume flew from their summits, and when the water vole surfaced, he was lost in a trough until he scrambled ashore, doubly drenched by a breaker. He threw a glance at the otter. Lut glimpsed the vole's terror, then the plump beast was safe, squeezing into his tunnel, and the other called fearfully. There was no sign of the bitch. The two cubs had gone.

Lut raced downstream. The sycamore trembled. Its skirts fluttered like a moth's wings, the strand swamped by creamers. But he found the holt empty. The emptiness numbed him, for he was sure they would have gone there, short of further disaster. Outside, the wind thundered. It took his breath. In a daze he returned to where he had left them. Demented air thrashed the bank. Shreds of willow herb scattered, the wild gardens pounded. There was no sign of the otters – just a single large boot print and a stick with blood on it, maybe Little Lut's.

The bitch had not waited. With two cubs tucked beside her she made for the nursery, leaving Lut to find the third cub. The gale moaned in trees and thickets. The whole vale was in uproar. Around the woods, poles capsized; laden boughs snapped and plummeted. Groups of deer shifted restlessly. At the Hall the wind screamed through the chimneys, ripping slates from the roof. They fell like axe blades. The gusts charged onto the ferry where the old apple tree toppled, drubbing down on the lean-to, part of which crumpled with it.

Bugle saw the sky writhing. Waves lifted then dropped her, and she nudged the cubs forward. They were struggling. She could not carry both and, reluctant to leave either, confined her efforts to goading. The holt was close yet seemed miles off. Then at last the rock loomed and she glimpsed the small landing, its awning in turmoil. The shaded strand had grown murky. She could make out gnarled roots, the black gape of the cavern, and urged her young through the shallows.

The next instant, she halted. Her eye had caught the dark tree bole where it rose from the grasses, and its line was distorted. Another shape bulged behind it. Her rasping huff was instinctive. The bulging profile drew closer, a fat and menacing figure. Bugle bolted. Snatching the nearest of her cubs, she fled back to the torrent, crossed the stream to the sedges and into the dyke which drained through them. Barely pausing, she pressed on down the cutting.

Duck had pitched there for shelter. As she flushed them, they were caught by the wind and flung sideways, forced to bat with the air stream. Steers raced crazily. Tails high, they kicked and bucked up a skyline where poplars bent like longbows. Wild-eyed, the bitch rested. The cub was heavy, no longer a suckling. Far off, the other cub called her. The

143

sound was plaintive but the first must be hidden before the second could be rescued. She went on urgently.

Dark eyes watched the burdened beast. The hare truckled. She had her own young in the meadow and was chary of intruders. Reassured by the otter's manner, the great doe kept her ears down, the wind anathema. Bugle passed; reached the culvert. It appealed as a bolt hole. Crawling in, she advanced to the far end and viewed the hill. At its top, dust whirled and spun as if the gritty clouds were living. There was a man in the farmyard. He seemed to tilt as he walked, leaning on the gusts.

Bugle sniffed. It was a new vista to the bitch, stark and blustery. Down the hedge a mob of young sparrows tumbled, summer's crop – a hawk with them. Both hawk and prey were gale-driven, the chase a lottery as sickle wings caught the turbulence, a small bird reprieved. Again the sparrow-hawk shafted. Bugle's gaze swept the stubble. Heads of rabbits rose from it, ears upright. They were not far from their buries. Every creature was twitchy and, in perfect sequence, the rabbits jumped for the hedgerow, their scuts disappearing. The bitch otter's eyes narrowed.

Three dogs were coming downhill. Two were collies, the third a lean wall-eyed lurcher. Wind in tail, they romped briskly, making darts at the rabbits and barking into the holes. There was a yelp. The cur had smelled the otters. In a trice they were beleaguered, dogs each end of the culvert, long muzzles panting. Bugle crawled to the centre. Cub beside her, she released her wrath fiercely, the low hiss explosive. The dogs snarled. Their rabbiting had been casual – the new mood was warlike, threats clashing mid-tunnel, brash overtures to battle. Teeth gnashed; claws scratched frenziedly.

For all of which, there was stalemate. The dogs could not force an entry; the otters were trapped there. Bugle spat with frustration. 'The wall-eyed lurcher is dangerous.' Lut had always proclaimed that, but she had fled from a greater danger, forced to leave a cub stranded, and she itched for its rescue. She moved to the drain's end. To foray was too risky, for the dyke's bilge was shallow, the dogs alert.

The wind screeched. It had dropped slightly; the draughts in the pipe were less uncomfortable. Pigeons winged now, the hawk hunting elsewhere, while nearby the hare stirred. For some while the doe had truckled, increasingly anxious. The dogs were close to her leverets and at last she lost patience. Rising artfully, she jogged up on the high ground until the yapping beasts spied her. Stilt-legged, she moved temptingly, bouncing, jigging, aware they could not resist her. And, to be sure, the otters suddenly bored them – with a hare to chase.

For a furlong the doe hung back to entice them, to draw them off from her infants, then showed her true paces. Frame flattened, low now as the stubble, she went away like an arrow, soon a field from her pursuers.

The otter listened. It seemed the yelping grew fainter and, perplexed, Bugle peeped from the hideout. The dogs were way up the hillside, all three brutes exhausted. Grabbing the cub, she dived swiftly from the culvert, sloshing back through the channel. Above the oaks, rooks were rising, still tossed in the airstreams, and she saw Corbie skulking, flying low near the play creek. By the river she whistled. The soft call was probing but brought no answer. In fear she crept closer, keeping deep in the sedges. She could see the rock as the stems swayed, and called again, bristling.

Something monstrous came downstream. A giant, it rode the current with arms flailing and Bugle flinched, the cub behind her. The apparition drove at them. Within a leap it swerved past, became a hugh bough of pinewood, and rolled on with the river. Smaller branches and twigs, lesser victims of the tempest, sailed with it. But, though Bugle kept calling, the second cub failed to join them and she grew more despairing.

'Bugle!'

She turned quickly, fangs glinting. The boy was running. At last he slid down the far bank. 'It's Little Lut, Bugle!' She huffed, no time for the urchin, yet relieved, for she had learned not to fear him. He was puffed by exertion. 'He's been killed – I've just found him. And I heard a cub calling.' The boy sat down, breathing tightly. He scanned the sedges, eyes urgent. At first he saw only Bugle, then, 'You've got one cub with you. I can see – tucked behind you. Where's the other?'

Lut arrived on the current. He was alone, agitated.

'For Pete's sake,' the boy pleaded, 'one's dead and one's missing! What's been happening? I heard a cub cry upriver.' A bitter call, hurt and frightened. The boy was shaking. 'I need the boat. I'm going to see,' he said huskily, 'find out what's happening. I'm going to find out what's happened to the other cub.'

Harn stepped into the river. Slowly, scarcely making a ripple, he prowled the shallows. Between each pace he froze briefly to peer through the surface. For a while he stalked catlike then, neck half extended, gazed intently at the water, remaining motionless. The heron was a statue. He moved, beak pointing. Again he froze. When at last he stabbed downwards, it was so swiftly he seemed barely to have twitched, the fish conjured from nowhere. It flapped a moment and was swallowed. Harn shook himself.

A chainsaw wailed. The heron scratched. Passing his beak through his chest plumes, the bird eyed the reach. The wind had gone. Only the saw broke the silence, a deep wounded stillness which sprawled like the flattened corn. Harn watched the ferry. Gradually, the fallen tree was diminishing, now piled as logs against the cottage. At length the man rested, sitting down on the log pile. He was listening. The faintest throb of a motor disturbed the ridge.

The boatman filled his briar, frowning. A car was approaching, winding down through the hedges. When it had stopped, she strode over. 'Heron's back,' said the woman. 'He wasn't here when I last called. The young must be on their own now.'

'Aye.' He said no more, brooding. She wore a frock beneath a jacket, and plain leather-strapped sandals. There was a man in the car. He sat looking straight forward as if the scene held no interest. The woman's gaze roamed over the cottage. 'Lost your tree. That's unfortunate. . . .'

'It'll burn.'

'Apple wood's nicely scented.'

'It smells.'

The boatman picked up the chainsaw. He looked past her to the car. Its occupant was expressionless, nose in a dossier. Scowling, the boatman triggered the handgrip and the chain screamed. As the log dropped, the woman seized on a silence. 'He's been here,' she asserted. If she was peeved, she concealed it. 'We've no doubt that he comes here and that someone befriends him.'

'The lad?'

She nodded. The man was sly as the youngster, and as truculent. She watched him stoop and the saw rasped. The heron stabbed downwards. This time the bird caught an eel, stalking ashore to kill the serpent. 'You know –' her voice had grown tighter, an edge to her composure '– it can't continue. He's more absent than present. You know he lies, that he's given false names?'

'I don't know what his name is.'

'But he comes here.'

The boatman spat. He knocked his pipe out. 'Find the beggar. It's your job.'

'Mr Kershaw intends to.'

'Mr Kershaw?'

'The department.'

'I'm busy.'

She checked her temper, chin rising. He could have been her grandfather. She must curb her authority, the impulse to be officious, the occupational hazard. All too easily it happened. She could become another Kershaw. The saw whined and a log dropped. She glanced askance at the car. Vale and river – Kershaw sat there, oblivious. His life was dossiers. The heron barked. Harn had flown, his yelp ringing.

He was resentful, thought the woman. She understood.

She and Kershaw were foreigners – to the bird, to the cottage. 'We're *all* busy,' she reproved with studied mildness, 'but we've social obligations. A child is absent.'

'Maybe best where he is.'

'And where is that?'

'Not here,' growled the boatman.

'I can see.'

'Ask yon otters: they might tell you.'

She caught the glint that he gave her. It was malevolent.

Splash! The boy shoved the dinghy out and scrambled onto her. She rocked, skimming through weed, then he was settled and rowing, pulling upstream. Oars flailed, brightly painted. It took a while to get their measure but soon he was coping – not, perhaps, as Hunter feathered, but compensating with effort for his lack of skill. No rebuke had assailed him. Across his shoulder he glanced forward. Rowlocks creaked.

'Come on, Lut, you can find her.' The missing cub was a female, a precious hope for the future. 'She can't be far from the river. We've got to come on her somewhere, and return her to Bugle.' Lut swam with the dinghy. The boy's sortie intrigued him. The otter bobbed near the vessel, sometimes ducking for minnows, but indifferent to the banks, though the other probed keenly. Rats hunched there, eyes mocking. 'Search, Lut. You don't know where we'll find her. You can't be sure.'

Lut seemed strangely lethargic. Maybe, the boy mused, the beast was stunned by the killing, the brutal death of the dog cub; perhaps resigned to further loss. Yet the lad did not think so. Lut was never a quitter. He had always been buoyant, indeed stubbornly hopeful. More likely the otter had his own methods and would search when sound or scent prompted, whereas the boy just kept looking. Ducking under low branches, he scanned the margins for the cub's spoor.

Mostly, the mud revealed birds' tracks. He saw the prints of snipe and redshank. Familiar arrows told of moorhens. Twice, the boy's hopes were quickened. The first time, the impressions were four-footed with curious drag marks. These marks flanked the footprints: on one side a thin line scored the silt; on the other a broader, less distinct line. Nothing of it meant otter. A mink had passed with her victim, a rat carried crossways, its head and tail dragging.

Farther on, a tunnel bored through tufty grasses. The hole was cub-sized and the boy landed. But other holes mined the grasses, the clump flattened at its centre, soiled with bird dung. Partridge had jugged there, forcing tunnels into their shelter. Now it was empty. Back in the boat, he rowed glumly. 'Come on, Lut, use your nose. She can't have got a lot farther.' *If* as far. He thought of Little Lut and shuddered.

Enraged, he jerked the oars wildly then, calming down, found a rhythm. A pair of swans called their cygnets. The cob busked, his wings threatening, while the pen led off downstream. A sandpiper flew low, skimming gale debris. Torn branches formed convoys. A plastic sack passed the dinghy, air in it, macabre as a floating corpse. At the weir the boy rested, gazing up at the torrent. No cub could have climbed it; he doubted Lut could have done so. He watched the spume fly.

At last, securing the vessel, the boy climbed the bank to the path behind the millhouse. Thickets almost engulfed it. He glanced at the otter. 'I'll take a look; she just might have come this way. Wait by the boat – I'll be back, Lut.' He saw the beast twist and dive. It was quiet, that long hush of late summer when few birds are singing, and the dim track was spooky. It emerged at the mill yard, a rank weed-strewn clearing amid crumbling buildings. Pigeons moaned and a door creaked.

The boy advanced, treading softly. The door hung where a shed rotted, its neglected roof gaping. Something moved in the bricks. He paused, startled by the wren which shot past him. He had disturbed its quest for insects. With a heave he swung the heavy door open, bent on searching the interior. The shed was not empty. In the gloom, the van seemed massive, almost touching the rafters, its tail towards the youngster. Beneath the grime he could still make out the word REMOVALS, and he turned to run, quaking.

Checking, he peered nervously around. He could hear voices. Again the boy verged on flight, instead entering the mill itself, where the gloom beckoned. He was at home now

150

in its entrails. Amid the cogwheels and spindles, joists and pulleys, he knew his way like a mill mouse. Flitting deftly through the rubbish, he gained the far window. From here he had watched Hunter. Chin close to the sill, he could see four men. All but one were by the building. They had found boxes to sit on while they boozed, their talk loud, laconic.

'We've not come here for sport.' He glimpsed the ferret-faced remover.

'Quit griping.' The fat hulk was conspicuous. 'I said I'd get me an otter.'

'It's a crime.' The third man spoke ironically.

The fourth stood nearer the pool. He tossed a can into the water. The big remover was cackling, a chilling sound, like a jay's braying laughter. He said, 'A crime? It's a kindness, taking care of an orphan.'

'The cub's never an orphan.'

'It can be fixed.'

'Yeah?'

'I'll orphan the beggar! She'll fetch a price in the smoke.'

'She won't live.'

'Until I've sold her, she'll live.'

The boy wriggled, hands sweating. At the pond the man was pounding the beer can, hurling half bricks at the water, smashing lilies and rushes. The fat man said, 'There were three. Lost the first when it bit me. Clumped the beggar; pulped it rotten. But I'm having the last one.'

'Fat fool,' snarled the ferret. 'If you foul up this outing. . . .'

'One more – that's an end.'

The boy shifted, fear mounting. Next, he heard the first stranger. 'Do we make it tonight?'

'If it's clear,' said the slight man.

'Or else?'

'When the cloud breaks.'

The second stranger said loudly, 'Rot this for amusement, let's get the job done with. I didn't reckon on this dump. Stuff his guts, and his otters, we're here for a share-out. We need the meat loaded.'

'Quit griping!'

The fat man eyed the box beside him. The sound of

scratching came from it. It was feeble but persistent. He kicked the box and it stopped. 'Don't you gripe, too, you beggar. I've heard enough griping. I'll fetch a boot to you.'

Beyond the weir, Lut had surfaced. Twice he swam around the boat as she tugged at her painter. No sign of the urchin – he pondered the footpath. The banks were still, thick with scrub wood and thistle. The otter listened. He might have heard the men's voices but for the sheeting cascade, whose roar was deafening. Instead he smelled them. On the breeze from the mill, which brought the scent of the she-cub, the otter smelled the removers and cursed their whole species.

Lashing fiercely through the fall, he gained the ledge behind the torrent. The plunging curtain entombed him. Countless tons teemed and thundered, spray drenching the chamber. Again he cursed, his coat streaming. Anguish tore him asunder: the urge to succour his daughter; his innate repugnance to man, the ancient enemy. The urchin was different. The boy had crossed the wild frontier. He was a friend and, encouraged by his proximity, Lut ran to the weir's end and climbed the bank.

Across the pool, the wheel cast its great reflection. Lut crouched in the bank growth. Now the voices came clearly. Diving quietly, he penetrated the depths towards the distant mill. There was a spot, thick with rushes, where he sometimes lay hidden. It was close to the buildings. The otter made for the shelter. Shoals of fish swam against him, flashing past in a hurry. Lut ignored them. He had one concern only, the hapless cub.

As he cruised he felt tremors. The speeding shoals sent out signals, but the shocks were not fish vibes; the waves were too violent. They explained why the fish fled, and Lut paused, spine tingling. Another quake rocked him sideways. Stems of lilies rose ahead. He glanced up. The round pads floated darkly and, while he watched, a sudden turmoil raged through them, blasting downwards and outwards, bubbles churning, leaves scattering. Slowly, the cause sank beside him: a brick from the mill bank, its impulse spent.

Lut retreated. Turning tail underwater, he sped from the missiles as swiftly as the fish, shooting the race to the catch

152

pool and safer depths. There, a blob in the deluge, he snarled frustratedly. Feet were thumping the footpath. The boy arrived at a gallop. 'They've got the cub!' He reached the dinghy, casting off. 'Four men,' he said, gulping, 'They've got the cub at the mill. We can't help her alone, Lut. I've got to warn Hunter. They'll come tonight.'

Great rods of rain swept the reaches, then passed, the sky clearing. The eve star had risen and a vixen came to water, ears pricked warily. She swung around. With a quick glance behind, she went away at a canter through the grey light. Bugle peered. The lithe fox left no word and the otter, midstream, could see no danger. It was Corbie who warned her. Guns were moving. Their barrels gleamed by the river as the crow sloped off darkly. 'Caw!' he bawled, stirring pigeons. Their wings clapped. A cock pheasant clamoured.

'Chrrr-cuk-cuk. . . .'

From the oaktops rooks scattered. Their flight was portentous, the oaring '*dread*' of the commune. It put the yaffle up, screeching; and alerted furred creatures. The jack hare hid in a plough voor, which his coat matched precisely. Shadows moved by the current. Bugle waited. There was a cough; a lewd oath, partly stifled. A stoat fled, red and sinuous. The bitch otter listened. 'Beware!' The 'dread' streamed above her and, where badgers' pipes surfaced, a grizzled snout vanished. Bugle dived to the sedges.

The rooks flew over the jetty. The cat eyed their black shapes then ran for the cottage. Inside, the man slumbered.

He awoke with a shiver, the room strangely dim, chair uncomfortable. He recalled it was evening. He had not eaten since breakfast, for he seldom took lunch, and his belly was grumbling. But his gut had not roused him. There was a sound. The inlaid wooden box shimmered. The boatman went to the kitchen. Something was trying to enter; something outside the cottage. He yanked the kitchen door open and the cat flew in, bristling.

Bugle made for the rock. She wished Lut could be with her, yet dared not call him. Shapes were moving. The bitch smelled the evil. In the reeds, the vole trembled as fear gripped the margin, stalked the bank by the woodside. Appalled, the water vole dithered. Should he swim or hold still? Grim shades towered and his pounding chest tightened at the roar of foul breathing. He crouched low, his eyes bulging. Where Otter Rock cast its shadow, the bitch had stopped.

Damply, she breasted the granite. Its unyielding touch braced her. Time had carved many fissures but left the stone solid, unbowed by the ages. She felt something of its history. Countless otters had swum there, dived and fished from the boulder. Cubs had romped on the summit. Old beasts had revived there. Once, unvanquished, Fingertaker had ruled the great rock. Here Lut's dam had been courted, and conceived her brood in swift water. It was a rock of survival. From that slab had trekked the last of the otters – to it Bugle had returned. Now she huffed in defiance.

Plunging fiercely to the holt, she crawled into the chamber. One cub remained, Little Lut's lonely brother, and she stood guard, eyes glaring. At all costs the bitch meant to protect him. In the gloom she was ugly. Her lips curled, her snout twisting. She could hear the removers. Their evil scent wafted, bringing threatening sounds with it. Mumbled words filled the tunnel. Something scraped the earthen passage, snagging roots as it worked its way closer, and she screened the cub, growling. Soil was crumbling. The cub whimpered. Next moment, the spear head of an ash staff, thrust suddenly, jabbed through the darkness and pierced the wall behind them.

As it withdrew, the fresh-cut tip took clay with it. The

155

probe hovered, vibrating, then stabbed again through the chamber. Bugle pressed back in horror. The cub was behind her, squeezed into a corner. This time, as the object lunged, she felt its point brush her flank, leaving earth on her guard hairs. There was a grunt down the tunnel. An obscene phrase came with it and now the rod juddered, jerked side to side so it plunged and whipped wildly, terrifying the otters. The chamber was lethal. Any moment one of the beasts would be gouged and Bugle's hoarse churr grew desperate.

'The back way!'

Pushing the cub, she pressed for the escape hole. The spear was jabbing. Dusk filtered from above and her young son stretched upwards. 'Wait!' Bugle restrained him. Her mistrust was well founded, for she saw the net plainly, stretched over the exit. She ducked back. They were trapped. Once more the cub whimpered and the sharpened rod pistoned. Bugle's anger rose viciously. In the fury of despair, she faced the probe with her fangs bared.

'The holt's empty.'

At the voice, she froze, listening.

'Not so sure,' spat the fat man.

'Come on, the others are ready.'

'Let 'em wait. It's too light yet.'

'I'm moving.'

The response was abusive. It rumbled underground and the spearing grew frenzied. Pain convulsed the bitch otter. She licked blood from her shoulder. It was a graze and she dodged the next onslaught, protecting her young one. 'Blamed otters!' There was a lull in the gouging. 'Rot 'em,' snarled the fat robber, 'they'll keep. Bloody vermin. Wouldn't bet they weren't in there.'

'Let's move. The herd's up wind.'

Bugle rested. For some time she lay quietly. The sounds had passed and the stench dispersed slowly. At last, creeping to the strand, she sniffed the evening. Clouds were shifting, dark skeins where the moon rose. Birds scuffled. At roost they stirred nervously. The hour was ominous. The bitch turned to her son. She nosed him gently, still laden with grief for her other cubs.

*　　*　　*

156

Hunter said, 'Come on, damn them!' He was hunched on a shooting stick close to the thicket, the old hound beside him. The boy had cramp. When it passed he said, 'They'll come.' He was frightened. The vale was patched with black outlines. Dusk lingered. Inky trees framed dim grazings as the silent deer drifted. Man and boy watched the herd feed.

By day the creatures had rested, chewing the cud, some beasts dozing. Now they dined, watchful, fidgety, graceful shapes gliding. A ten-pointer stood proudly, the stag's handsome head lifted. Hunter said, 'Let 'em come, boy – they'll rue it.' He had seen the work of such vandals, the beasts left wounded, gaping holes in the creatures, legs shattered. He loaded his shotgun. It was done with fierce relish and the lad's thin nape tingled. The urchin stiffened. A tiny grass spider touched him.

The men were moving. Somewhere, he thought, they were shifting, but the hushed vale seemed lifeless, summer spent, autumn waiting. Leaves clung stiffly to coverts. Though still green, their supple moistness had drained away until they looked cold and sculptured, the woods themselves time-locked. Within them night was deep already. It was the darkest of their seasons and the boy pondered woodpaths, black and lonesome, great ivy-wrapped columns. They came to mind with strange intensity, as if his senses were heightened. He could feel them – feel the nearby stream's slither, smell the mill, hear the she-cub's soft sobbing. 'The cub. . . .'

'Quiet, boy.'

'They shan't have her.'

'Keep your voice down.'

'They mustn't.'

'B'God,' Hunter said harshly, 'it's the deer they want, damnit. One thing at a time!'

'You won't let them take her?'

The man scowled. His eyes tightened. They ached as the light failed. 'You're sure it's tonight?'

The boy nodded.

'Then keep looking. They'll come up from the river by that fold in the rise. They'll want dead ground and the wind in their faces. Your sight's good, boy; you'll spot them.' Hunter blinked in the gloaming. At the boy's age he could see in the dark, had prowled by night with the keepers. *Then* it was different. An aircraft hummed, its lights winking. That was new in his lifetime. He recalled the first to pass over, stampeding deer and cattle. A bag of string with an engine. *Then* the Hall had been staffed, a small army employed there.

'Look. . . .' The child's voice disturbed him.

An owl swept the grazing, and another, pale and wide-winged. They swirled out of the gloaming, wheeled and vanished, the second being the whiter, a fledgling of the night trade. The older owl had seen something. A thin scream crossed the dew, the last cry of a mouse.

'Bah!' said Hunter. He scanned the blurred woodside. The oaks seemed unchanging. A few were bald now on top, providing perches for kestrels; a few had sprung up in hedges along with beech and ash striplings. Thorn had thickened with age, become brighter with berry. Much remained loyal to memory. Copse and brake still gave shelter; old pasture glowed patchily. Only where willows had seeded, their roots near water, had dimensions changed greatly, like those of a child who grows suddenly.

Hunter glanced at the urchin. 'Any signs?' There was no answer. 'Don't worry, you'll spot 'em.' He smiled, a gaunt glimmer. The young scamp had done well, come up trumps with his snooping. The gun twitched, the man's ancient hands shaking. 'Bear up, boy, we'll teach 'em!'

'Maybe,' the boy whispered.

'*Maybe*?'

'I mean – there's four men to tackle.'

'Damned riff-raff.'

'They're geared for night hunting.'

'Thieving, blast it! By thunder,' snarled Hunter, 'I fought two wars. Do you think I can't face them? Damn your nerve, I'll rout 'em!' There was silence. 'You young beggar.' It was softer. 'I'm not blasted done for. We'll celebrate later. You'll need a roof. Not short of rooms at the Hall – you can billet there.'

'I'd not mind, but. . . .'

'It's settled.'

'The boatman has asked me.'

'Damned old fool. You can't stay with that beggar.'

'With neither of you,' the boy said. 'They'd find me. Kershaw's watching.'

Hunter said, 'He'd not take you from *me*, boy.' He liked the lad; he had spirit. 'Let him try. I'd adopt you.' It slipped out unconsidered. Hunter savoured the notion. 'How would that be?' he mused, going on with gruff affection, 'You need a home and you'd still have the otters. I'd have someone to fish with.' A young man growing up there; new blood in the old place. 'How would that suit?'

'You'd do it?' the boy said. Moonlight silvered the mansion. 'I'd have a home on the river?'

'It would answer, young fellow.'

'You and me?'

'And the hound.'

'We'd save the otters?' The boy's eyes glowed like a wild thing's thought Hunter. 'I can't leave them,' the child said. 'I belong with the fishers – they've returned and they've bred. I prayed for that in the marsh church: for a real otter river. But already they're threatened. One cub's dead and one's taken.'

'We'll protect them.'

'Save the she-cub?'

'Don't fret.' Hunter tensed. The dog had growled, a low deep-throated rumble. 'What's that?' the old man said, head turning.

The boy saw only the landscape. The deer were blobs now, a ghost herd. Black trees rose from moon planes and a mist had crept upstream, its grey tendrils spreading. Hollow gicks shoved up near him. They clawed the stars, brittle hands of a dying summer. They obscured the boy's vision. He gazed around them, thought spinning. Make his home with the recluse? A stag coughed, the sound rasping. At the Hall? He was dazed. He tried to think. 'Come on, boy! Can you see them?'

'No,' he said in confusion. He looked again, his mind clearing. 'Wait. . . .' His sight pierced the gloom, straining down through the gully. There was a glint. He saw the gleam of a barrel, then a dim, stooping figure – and, nearby, another. For a moment he lost them, the shapes enveloped in shadow before they tracked across clear ground. 'Three,' he

159

muttered. 'In the hollow. Three now. They've got guns.'
They passed into the fold and he said, his spine icy, 'You
won't glimpse them until the wood's end.'

'Then I'll have 'em!' said Hunter.

'They'll be close.'

'Where I want 'em.'

'Should be four,' the boy whispered.

Hunter said, 'Damn the numbers; just listen, young
fellow.' He grasped the boy's shoulder. 'See the spinney?
You can nip round behind it, reach the Hall under cover. I
want you in the house quickly. Until this job's done, you'll
stay there.'

'I'm helping. . . .'

'In the house, boy.'

'You need help.'

'Push off, blast you!'

The boy went, pausing guiltily. Looking back he saw the
nine-fingered ancient outlined near the bushes – one against
the removers. His own relief on leaving shamed him. 'Take
care, Hunter.' The words, too late, stuck inside and he
hauled himself away dumbly. Scudding clouds screened the
sky-ceiling. He groped on through black void until stars and
moon glistened, then hugged the fir plantation. A curlew
cried and bats winnowed.

He felt the draught of thin wings, his perception acute
now. He smelled strange, menacing fungi; heard the scuttling of shrewmice. He had an otter's awareness, a wild fear
of gunfire, and ran frantically.

The Hall glowered. Its great pile scowled from black mullions across rough moon-blanched gardens, unkempt as the woodlands, and the boy halted, panting. An old fence rotted. Yew hedge, once trimly fashioned, formed a now shaggy frame around monochrome rose plants and lawns rucked with mole runs. He climbed the fence, resting briefly on gravel. The drive was dark, densely sheltered. For a moment he faced the Hall, eyes lingering, then turned away. When he glanced back the house was hidden by rampant shrubs.

Pebbles crunching, he ran on towards the ferry, the vale ahead. A light burned, a mere chink on the landline. It glowed deep yellow, unlike the far sweep of marshes which, star-domed, seemed frosted. The boy thought of winter. He recalled the snow falling and the aged punt ice-bound. He recalled the marsh woman. '*Otters, is it! You're too late. . . . Doomed as dodos . . . all God's blessing of beasts. . . . There'll be a reckoning.*' He stopped a second time, winded. Gulping breath, he dragged on to the cottage and thumped the door.

Nothing happened. He leaned against the wall, gasping. Again he thumped, standing back as he recovered. The place was in darkness. He called under a window. Unanswered, he seized the door latch. It turned freely and he groped for a switch, shedding 100-watt lamplight. The kitchen was scruffy. Dirty crocks lay about and a mug held some coffee. The stuff was cold. He went into the parlour. It was tidier. His eye was drawn by the ship-box. Flipping the lid, he took out the old photo and stared at its image. He put it back. The stolid sepia boy meant nothing to him. There was no affinity. He called once more, this time up the small staircase, then ran outside.

He breathed deeply. The misty vapour was welcome. The empty cottage had scared him, its rooms strangely oppressive. His nerves were taut and he sensed that he was watched. He heard a crunch. The sound was soft, as if puny bones were breaking. There was a hiss. Two brilliant eyes fixed him and he saw the cat eating. He had not known it so hostile. Resentful, he cursed it, stepping quickly to the jetty. Reeds droned, the stream driving. Its smell was thick, damp and weedy, and another came with it, the scent of burning tobacco.

'It's you, boy!' The boatman emerged from the mist. The child's slight figure surprised him. For an instant, from the bank, he had thought an animal stood there, half glimpsed in the vapour. 'You all right? You look harried.'

'The men – they're climbing the slope.'

'Calm down, lad.'

'The removers!' The urchin's arm pointed. 'Up there. Hunter's waiting. He's on the ridge, in the thorn brake. Alone there.'

'Blamed madman!'

'They'll kill him.'

'Take a lot to kill Hunter.'

The boatman yanked his cap forward. Puffing smoke, he lurched up to the cottage. 'Blamed warmonger!' He spat, crossing the garden. The boy followed. Trellised beans threw spiked shadows. 'The pigheaded tyrant!' They approached the wrecked lean-to. A small shed was still standing. 'It's been the same, boy, for centuries. His lot scrap and the likes o' me joins 'em. Bloody Hunters, the crackpots!' He went into the hut. 'Not two beans to his name and the man's turned down millions.'

162

'For the land?'

'Development.'

'They'd ransack it.'

'Tree and beast.' The boatman brought out a pitchfork. 'Why else would I save him?' He stuffed his pipe in a pocket. The mist swirled. 'I'll be back.' He turned stiffly. 'And I don't want you with me, d'you hear? That's an order!'

There was no word. This time the boy did not protest, for the stream's voice was clear and he knew his own mission. Instead he watched the man go, then slipped down to the sedges. Somewhere, mallard were quacking. The noise resounded. He heard the 'whee-oo' of wigeon. Trout lay in deep hideouts. At dusk they had guzzled; now they skulked amid weeds and in the riverbed debris. A score lurked under the jetty, whose supports offered bunk holes. The boy knew their places. He knew the hiders and those who did not seek cover but simply lay on the bottom, camouflaged by their livery.

Breasting reeds, he fared up river. His feet squelched. The mist hung low in weird strata, nosing dankly into ditches. Pools gurgled. With a shriek, a late snipe left the mud, flighting south for the marshes. Where Hunter's banks gave firm footing, he ran on grass beneath great oaken caverns until, reaching the boathouse, he looked for the dinghy. The craft was not at her mooring. He tried the doors of the building. They were locked. In frustration, he shook them but they held against force. He would have to push his way up to the mill on foot.

As he advanced, brambles snagged him. The banks grew wilder, more tangled, each step bringing problems. Often, wading was the answer. Once he swam, his way blocked by deep water, but mostly he scrambled, shoving tight-lipped through thickets and sloshing through reedbeds. Time was short. He had to reach the cub quickly. And as he struggled he listened for the gunshot he dreaded – the opening shot.

The imprisoned cub whimpered. It was quiet now, the men gone, and she lay in the dark. For short spells she had slept, overwhelmed by fear and misery. Only sleep offered comfort. Even that was tense and fitful, remote from natural slumber. In the holt she would lie stretched out with Bugle.

163

There, her floppy coat puckered and she oozed relaxation. Now, small nose thrust in tail, she slept tautly and shuddered, giving bleats of unhappiness. Awake, it was worse, for the nightmare persisted: the bare wooden cell she could not escape.

She had tried to do so. At first, in terror, she had scratched the walls until her claws bled. She had gnawed wood in her panic. But while her teeth made scant impression, the splinters did, her mouth suffering. At length, exhausted and wretched, she had taken stock. Above, a small hole let in air. By day, a streak of light shone there, retracting at evening. Then moist breath filled the dungeon and she craved the dusky freedom.

With every nerve she yearned for Bugle. The cub's cry was woeful. River, holt, stars and sedges: her whole world was denied her. Sounds came strangely. The weir's roar bemused the prisoner, constant as her desolation. At least she could smell water. She put her nose in a corner. The old wood had warped slightly, split at the angle, and her forepaws explored it. It gave a fraction. Encouraged, the cub scratched the opening, tearing slivers from the edges. For some time she gnawed and worried, then cowed down, hearing footsteps.

A man turned the corner. He came round the mill, mumbling, clutching a beer can, and stopped by the pond. 'Come on,' he urged the absent removers, 'you're slow.' He hurled the can in the water. There was no shooting. When the fourth man heard shooting, he would drive the van forward. Meanwhile, the place made him jumpy. He veered away round the building and the cub heard him swearing. 'Christ, you're slow!' She could hear his feet scuffing. 'Come on, you clodhopping butchers, what's keeping you?'

When the noise had abated she gnawed again. The job was painful for the wood chafed, pieces jabbing her muzzle, but she toiled patiently. At last, exhausted, she rested. The aperture was still tiny, little more than a spyhole through which she saw the millpond. The view itself was a torment. She looked on reeds and smooth water, the curving dip at the weir's edge. She saw the moon and every instinct screamed in her to be released.

Then, as she watched, the pond rippled. The little otter's heart quickened. A broad head had pushed upwards, towering under the vapour. It turned, scanning the bank, fierce brow dripping, submerged and rose nearer. The cub squealed. Wildly, she tore at the spyhole.

Grass rustled and Lut, leaving the water, reached the box with swift movements. He made no sound. Twice, he skirted the container appraising its construction, then set his teeth to the fissure. Wood split as his jaws wrenched. Inside, the cub toiled, hopes soaring.

Tearing, spitting, Lut laboured. The wood was hard. He paused to listen, head lofted. For several minutes he worked before, alarmed, he took cover. The man was moving. Lut dived, swimming quietly to the rushes, from where he heard the man cursing. The animal waited. Then a voice came much nearer. 'Lut?' The tall stems waved gently. 'Is that you?' the boy whispered. Lut saw a face scratched by brambles; the drenched clothes of the urchin.

'Keep still, Lut, I'm with you. Don't worry, we'll get her. When the man leaves, be ready. Stay in the pool, I'll release her.' The boy wriggled forward. 'He's going back. Be ready to call her, Lut.'

The dog otter trod water. He could just see the boxes, hear the man's clumsy movements. The boy was crouching, running doubled, ducking under scrub willow. Lut held back then, as the other reached the mill, surged from the reeds, prow-wave spreading. The big wheel creaked. The otter's snout dipped and vanished. Near the building, he surfaced, peering cautiously landward. The boy was searching the boxes. 'It's gone,' he breathed, 'the man's moved it. This lot are empty. He's moved her, Lut.'

The child groaned. Hair-thin legs brushed his forehead. He swiped at the insect. It cruised on, a crane fly, limbs dangling. Others whirled in the starlight. Springing up from the turf, they filled the evening in thousands, celebrating their transformation, the hour of rebirth. The boy batted them off.

'Stay here, I must find her.' He inched his way to the mill yard.

Damp and cold, he paused in doorways. The night was

mild. He owed his coldness to fear. The man was somewhere in the buildings, and every noise could startle. A rat moved amid rubble. Overhead, sparrows scuffled, knocking dust from the masonry where they slept. He passed a dull, cob-webbed window. Something budged and he halted, eyes reluctantly attracted. The crane flies danced dimly. Flying in through a door they had reached the glass pane and found their way out obstructed. Through the window he watched them. Not long ago they were earthbound, now slender wings bore them up, their old shapes divested. Half a dozen gangling prodigies. The boy hugged a shadow. Scuttling quickly to another, he found himself at the back of the ruin, the van ahead of him.

It had been moved from the shed and stood out on bright cobbles. The man, he thought, must be in it, but as the urchin sneaked closer the cab appeared to be empty. He tucked in by a rain butt. The chill had gone: he was sweating. He felt the warmth at his armpits. Gritting, he peeked round the barrel and scanned the yard. There were blind spots. He could not see behind the van or fully into the cabin, but the place *felt* deserted. It was no time to ponder. Stooping, he made a rush for the vehicle and pressed his back to it.

For a second he waited then moved slowly sideways to the driver's door. He eased the handle. His wet rags had smeared the panel. The grime was sludgy. The door opened and, craning in, he saw only empty seats until, shaking with apprehension, he climbed higher, dropped back to the cob-bles and peered round the yard. He had found the box. It was in the well on the passenger side, amid a plethora of litter. He eyed the buildings. There was no sign of the driver and he dodged round the cab to the other door. As he yanked it, there was a squeak from the container. He was not the only one frightened, he told himself.

'All right, Lut's waiting,' he said quietly. 'We'll take care of you.' He heaved the box. It was heavy. The boy placed it on the ground. He needed a lever to wrench the wood.

The yard had darkened. Misty cloud wreathed the mill and the cobbles grew leaden. He cast vainly in corners, vision foiled by the gloom. A new wave of fear swept him. Vital seconds were passing. There was no time to search for tools and, grasping the box, he balanced its weight. The moon returned with sudden brilliance. It bathed the rain butt and walls, swamped the stones and, to cap the boy's terror, revealed the man by the building. For a moment both were startled. The yard's width lay between them. A starry stillness had settled and in that brief intermission the gunshot rang.

The echoes travelled. In rolling volleys they swept the woods and crossed meadows, rousing pheasants and farm dogs. The vale stirred; fell silent. The boy moved first. As the sound died he clasped the box to his ribs and ran for the river. The path led downwards through trees, snarled by growth. The child stumbled, top heavy. Still afoot, he reeled forward. He could hear the man pounding. The laden fugitive galloped. Sounds of crashing pursued him, grunts of fury and exertion. Flanking the weir, he reached the stream, his burden now overwhelming.

There was a flint near the river. Lodging the box on the bank, he raised the stone. Its teeming underworld scattered. The man was blowing. The boy plied the crude hammer. Smashing the top of the container, he tipped it over. Nothing happened. Then, in a flash, the cub scrambled free, flopping into the water. Lut was waiting, swirling round the smaller otter. The driver snarled. Arms reaching, the man lunged but the boy had gone, leaping outwards, diving after the sleek fishers. The flow enveloped him. He swam submerged with the current, kicking lazily.

Ahead, the otters were gliding. They seemed to drift in green moonlight, ineffably graceful. He followed weightlessly. Fronds from deep gardens stroked him. Bubbles soared. He felt safe. Lut turned back, ghosting easily around him, his snout solicitous. Abreast now, the three headed downstream.

Atop the ridge the boatman rested. A bizarre figure jigged there, hopping gauntly from bush to thicket. It was, the other thought, a devilish, crazed apparition. He half expected a donkey's ears on it, but only Hunter's creased face leered at him. *Bang!* The devil fired skywards, then again. The view below them was luminous. Marsh and valley merged mistily in witness to this demon who pranced on the high ground. Black geese cronked. Fattening lambs stirred on marsh grass.

Bang!

Far off, the sea was crashing on shingle with violent appetite.

The boatman watched, wheezing. Many times had he stood there, clouds driving like greyhounds. He had grown up on the flats, between meadows and saltings. It was a land of apparitions, a strange place where winds howled and the sea fogs rose swiftly. You could be lonely, glad of God, on the marshes. Curlews cried and gulls drifted. Unseen ships moaned in passing, phantoms of the horizon; and when he was younger, topsails had crossed the pastures, hauling up to the wool wharf. He belonged there, like Hunter. Unlike Hunter, he had kept his sanity.

Bang! The wild man reloaded.

The boatman braced himself, pitchfork levelled. 'Where are they?'

'In the coombe. I warmed their ears for the beggars.'

'You're mad, Hunter.'

'Shoot and move, that's the ruse! They think they've met a battalion.'

'Hold fire, you blamed madman.' Same blood-and-guts Hunter! He had always been violent: setting hounds at damned otters; blasting off with his punt gun. The boatman thought of the old times, the great floods of past winters when valley and marsh drowned. Then hares sat in pollards and foxes had climbed haystacks. That was the time of migration, duck and geese on raw pinions. Then the otters had whistled, filled the nights with their business while crows moped in treetops. Then a great peace would settle, the deep hush of inundation, and a boatman was someone of value.

As was Hunter, the squire's son. Not for Hunter, tranquillity. The floods for him had meant shrapnel, gunsmoke in the reedbanks. Blood and thunder! The blamed fool had not changed since first they swapped insults. Now the boatman said, 'Hold it, you can't afford the rounds, mister. You've stampeded the deer; they'll be out of it safely behind the Hall. Just tread softly.'

'I'll stampede the damned ruffians!'

'Keep quiet and let's place them.'

'In the coombe.' Hunter scowled. 'You're late, damn it. They're in the coombe, I just told you.' He snapped the breech of the shotgun. The deer had gone, that was certain. The fusillade had alarmed them, sent them off through the birches, bouncing over the brambles to the oak-studded park, where a big hind had led them down the long wall to cover, safe even from rifles. Hunter pressed home two shells. 'There are three men below us. We'll rout them, the beggars. They'll not return quickly.'

The boatman restrained him.

Hunter whirled. 'Charge, you dotard!'

'Maniac! We can't see them.'

'I say, charge. . . .'

169

'When they move – maybe then, you blamed halfwit.'
They peered over the thicket, two old men with gun and
pitchfork. Dark leaves roofed the incline. Beyond, the stream
twinkled; much farther, creeks shimmered. Out there, where
the tide crept, oozing, swirling on the mud flats, wildfowl
clanged and seals grunted. The boatman smelled the salt
breeze, the pod wrack in the breakers. The restless flow
beckoned. He said, 'No sign. They've been rumbled. They'll
beat it.'

'When I reach 'em! Bring that hound, we're advancing.'

'Blamed old fool.' But he followed, lurching after the
other, fork grasped like a pikestaff. Hunter's stooped back
grew dim. They were groping through woods whose dark
paths had known pikemen. Lichened hornbeams were
ancient; the oaks seemed antler-headed. Withered limbs
clawed the gloom, fossilized on live torsos with roots like sea
monsters. The shotgun probed shadows best ignored,
thought the boatman, for the coombe was not friendly. Men
once called it a witch wood, a queer place. Many wild
creatures shunned it.

'Blast the murk,' Hunter growled. 'Keep up, fellow, we're
near 'em.'

'You may think so. I doubt it.'

'Where's the dog?'

'Fallen out.' And with good sense, mused the speaker. Few
beasts liked the coombe. You might hear an owl hoot there, a
she-weasel scold, but no rabbit lived long in that ossified
covert, nor were squirrels part of it. Only pheasants
abounded, without the wit to be frightened. 'Aye, fell out,'
snarled the pikeman, shuffling sullenly forward. 'Dog's more
sense than us, Hunter. Knows his age. You and me, we're
not striplings. Too old. . . .'

'Speak for yourself!'

The boatman stopped. 'What was that?' He stood listening. 'Did you hear? There – twigs cracking!'

'A badger.'

'Like hell! Yon's no badger. They're making down to the
river; pulling out, as I reckoned.'

Hunter said, 'You're right, damn it!' He cocked the gun,
face distorted with triumph. 'Come on, after the beggars!

170

B'God, they're running like rabbits; we'll pepper their arses!'

'Let 'em go. I'm off back.'

'You can't mutiny now, man!'

'Let 'em run.'

'Chase and harry. . . .'

'Home, mister.' The boatman peered into shadows thick with gnarled boles and branches. Ivy bolstered the darkness, sombre leaves shrouding tree stumps, creeping snakelike from thorn tombs, the black maws of thickets. The coombe was a necropolis. Countless creatures had died there, transfixed by cruel winters. Ancient scrub hid their bones: spindlewood, butcher's broom. Ghosts made sounds where the draughts blew. 'I'm for home; the boy's waiting.'

'The boy's safe at the Hall.'

'At the cottage.'

Hunter turned. 'You mean, he went to the ferry?'

'Left him there,' said the boatman.

'Blast the brat, you can't trust him.' Hunter's triumph had vanished. 'Now see what he's up to, how his devious mind works. Damned otters! He's hoodwinked us, gone up the river. He'll run into these ruffians.'

'Blamed youth!'

'Are you coming?'

'I am, mister.'

Fast water! It streamed in twisting sinews as they fled the weir's rumble. The rescued cub paddled bravely. Lut urged her downriver then dived through the current to rise where the boy swam. Lut's confidence returned. The mill was gone; the stream led to safety. He surged in the water. Ahead, the rock beckoned. Plunging deep, the otter sloughed off his tensions, soothed by fronds in hushed gardens, rejoining the she-cub.

The stream would not fail him. Soon its coils would turn to gold, reflecting the autumn, and rains would renew it. With first flood came the eel run. The otters would guzzle. From the rock, Lut had gleaned the eel harvests, robbed the silver armadas. Now Bugle would feast there, and her cubs – and, in time, their own offspring. Lut trusted the river. His ancestors had fished there. He felt good with his daughter.

171

Wavelets slapped and their spume flicked. Abeam, black walls, palisades of spiked reed mace held the night from the swimmers. They escaped down Lut's highway. It sped and thrust with them, an age-old route racing on into fog banks. Theirs was a raking perspective, the view of the bank vole. The reeds were its limit. Wood and ridge were beyond; paths were hidden. They saw neither the bog grass nor the marksman who stood there.

The fat man's eyes narrowed. The night was a washout. The place was dead, devoid of deer, and he glimpsed nothing smaller. A pheasant railed but it was distant, disturbed at roost by another. He snarled, stomping forward. The tufts of grass glimmered moistly. As he advanced, he flushed crane flies. They blurred the man's vision, grey and spindly, like liverish images, and he swiped at them, grunting. A wan mist curled and drifted. Something bobbed on the river. The vapour swirled, then another shape surfaced. He lifted the rifle.

Reeds chattered. The gun was power, slim and potent. He watched the seaward-bound water, tongue in lips, his gross frame firmly anchored. Mist and current joined dimly. For a while he was thwarted by the opaque, clinging dampness – but the elements parted and he stared down the barrel. Again the dark shapes broke surface. Slick and flat, they came and went in the gunsight, side by side – swimming otters. Their wakes were visible, first two then a third.

He filled the sight with a target. The gun was vengeance. It redressed the injustice: their lithe, skimming beauty. The target slid out of focus. He framed the next dusky blob, let it vanish. The third was larger and painstakingly he held it. The air was murky. The marksman lingered. He scarcely heard the emission. The report was sharp, unlike the bark of a shotgun, and he peered at the vapour.

'Christ,' a voice said, 'you hit him!'

His slight companion lurched forward. 'Jesus Christ,' he cried hoarsely, 'it was a kid – a boy swimming!'

The fat man looked puzzled.

'He went under. I saw the kid – Christ, you hit him!'

'I missed. It was an otter.'

The marksman lowered the rifle. The other grabbed him,

voice frantic. '*You hit him*! Don't stand there, we've got to do something. . . .' He fell backwards, shoved away, sprawling into the rushes. The fat man said, 'They were otters,' his eyes on the river. He knew the brutes when he saw them. In his time he had killed most things, birds and beasts, but not kids. 'It was an otter,' he rasped. 'In any case, I've not been here. Where's the van? We've not been here, none of us.'

The other rose, his face ghostly. 'It's dark,' he conceded. 'Mist plays tricks.'

'I could have sworn. . . .'

'We've not been here.'

The scrawny man nodded. 'You could be right; you could have missed.' He glanced nervously around. There was nothing on the water. It would drift. A floating object would drift a long way by the morning. 'Van's in the lane. We've done nothing. We've touched no deer, there's no harm done.' He was shaking. 'The gun. . . .'

'I'll take care of the rifle.'

'Not here.'

'I'm not stupid!'

Lut slid out from the bank. He had dived under its shoulder, to emerge as the men went. He could hear their tones fading. Another sound reached him, the low cry of the cub, and he sought her location. The bleat spanned the water. It skirled feebly from the far shore, a tremulous summons. He crossed the stream to the sedges. They swayed and droned but now the small beast was silent. Lut called softly. Apprehensively he waited, then the bleat was repeated. He pushed through the stems, snuffling.

She lay in the shallows. Head and shoulders were dry, her feet gripping the bottom. The flow eddied round her. On Lut's arrival, she whimpered, neck stretching. He loomed darkly, his wide-set eyes anxious, thin mud streaming from him. Unmoving, he listened. It was quiet. With a dart he snatched the cub by the scruff, hauled her clear of the water and sprang ashore. She was uninjured. He nosed her along on her own feet.

She ran a few steps and halted. The dog otter chivvied. Fiercely, he drove the weary cub downstream until trees overhung them and the great rock towered dimly. They

173

swam the last stretch together. Home surroundings recharged her and she raced for the tunnel. At the strand the dog waited. He watched her crawl through the trellis, heard the holt's muffled music, squeals of joyous reunion. The cubs and Bugle were exultant. Lut turned to the water.

It stretched away into blank mist. The flow barely whispered. For a long time he waited. He strained his ears but caught only the soft slap of water, the endless chant. The night deepened. Just once he thought the boy was calling, but it was Hunter, his voice distant. Slowly Lut climbed the incline and went inside.

Two herons flew over. The day was warm and their flight indolent. The big birds ambled until one dived aerobatically, the other pursuing. Then, climbing, they flew on again. They were young, the air heady. Their first winter was coming but of that they knew nothing. Life was good. Self-importantly, they shouted. The stream was theirs, they asserted. 'A heron river!' the first yelped.

'Beyond doubt,' screeched the second.

'The removers have fled.'

'The boy no longer disturbs us.'

A single tree had turned amber. It stood out like a beacon. Soon others would follow – hazel, beech, birch and maple – until the shoalbacked ridge flamed, the oaks alone merely smouldering. But still summer's rump lingered. Marjoram bloomed; ring doves crooned. On the brambles, the gaudy red admiral showed his spinnakers. Lut set course for the wharf. The old quay would lie full in a welcome sun.

It was an odd time, this halting onset of autumn. The clear white light gleamed on spiders; dewy nights feared frost's ambush. Yet by noon it was balmy, recalling spring with strange vividness. In the fields the grass thickened, woods glowed green where the sun pierced through. Birds flirted. Rooks and robins grew mettlesome. Somehow, it seemed, the ghosts of May had awakened for the flowering of ivy, the reddening of holly in Hunter's wood. The ghosts stirred memories.

Lut heard echoes of springtime: '*The cubs have come, Lut – for Pete's sake!*' He recalled the small bundles, squirming, mewling. A dwarf image glimmered – the wobbling swagger of Little Lut. Now the dog otter floated. The warmth lulled him as he paddled, and he let the stream take him, diving nearer the jetty to rise beyond the cottage. Here the rushes were tawny. They brought back his own cubhood. The boy would sit in those rushes, catching fish for the otter.

'*Here, Lut, here's a big one!*'

He remembered.

The otter blinked. Tall stems were rocking. Across the stream the ripening seed pods of ragwort parachuted in clusters. A mild western draught bore them, but it could not have swayed the reed mace, whose brown heads were nodding, and Lut approached with cautious interest. Yarrow grew near the margins, and trembling harebells. Sinking all but watchful eyes, he drifted quietly. Water sloshed. Something stood in the shallows, concealed by the dense vegetation. Lut huffed warily.

With a leap, a large creature broke cover. The deer had been drinking. She traipsed away, the reeds closing, and Lut swirled on, disappointed. At the wharf he left the current, climbing up to the brickwork. Moss matted the rampart. Lut dripped on saffron-hued lichens, the water trickling to niches where old cement crumbled. He looked out to the marshes, recollecting the punt trip. Here he had first crossed the frontier.

'Poacher's luck, Lut!' Harn was hunched in the sedges. 'Poacher's luck won the marsh bitch.'

Lut turned to the heron.

'Boldness, Harn!' That, and help from the boy, if he had to be truthful, but that was not for Harn's hearing. Lut made steps for the bothy. Summer's tangle enmeshed it, the growth dying back now. Rank nettles had withered, teasel and burdock turned brittle. The slender voice of a wren

176

trilled. One patch remained barren, stubs of burned wood still on it. The boy had crouched there, face ruddy, the sparks and smoke rising. Lut would not forget quickly.

He entered the brick hut. A clutch of haws, stored by fieldmice, lay in a corner. The otter sniffed the dark shelter. It held no sign of occupation save the berries and a long-empty bean can, devoid now of odour. He returned to the sunlight. Once the old punt had wallowed where dragonflies hovered. He recalled the boy's anguish. *'Don't forget, Lut, we're pals. You can't push off. We're together.'*

The boy had saved him – and the she-cub. Now gnats swarmed and Lut slouched to the water. Harn had gone. The otter peered through the surface.

Dace and roach moved beneath him. At first he saw just a few, olive shades in deep gardens, then the shoal caught the sun and a great army glittered. It jerked Lut back to business. Some of the small fish were rising then flicking down with brisk movements, but the big ones swam smoothly, their fins barely twitching. Their march was unhurried and he let them pass before diving, turning after the stragglers.

Lut knifed the tide's shoulder. As the green flow enclosed him he stabbed for its core, slicing steeply through weed, past the wharf's sunken face to the rock-littered gully. He could see the fish ahead. Keeping low, he stalked the horde, drawing closer. The drowned hulk of the barge loomed. The otter threaded its wreckage, sheering nimbly through dunes and vegetation until he reached the finned rearguard. Fry glittered above him. Among them, holding steadily to course, the big fish of the shoal streamed in glossy lines.

Lut picked a target. He waited. A willow dappled the surface, obscuring the swimmers, then a clear ceiling framed them. He surged upwards, neck flexing.

But his quarry escaped him. As he rose, the shoal scattered, spreading out like a starburst. Roach and dace fled on all sides, large and small, their scales flashing. Lut watched them, bewildered. Darts of light, they whipped past him. He glimpsed the mighty fish leader, then in scores the horde faded, streaking out of his vision. In the depths Lut paused, wondering. They had not seen him coming, of that he was certain. Something else had upset them.

177

A throbbing roar filled the water. The otter stared. The stream was churning, bubbling, the pulse growing stronger. He dived. A black shadow swept over and the flow became violent, silt rising in flurries. Lut swam blindly to the bank. There, he could see the boat plainly. It chugged away down the river, wash slopping around him, and he heard distant voices. Other sounds crossed the levels: a shout, a dog whining.

Lut climbed the bank. It was quiet and he thought sheep-dogs might be working, fetching ewes from the meadows. A drab pall smudged the skyline. The cloud was moving in slowly, trailing rain like grey lambs' tails. He contemplated the water. The shoal could still be near the wharf and he made for that structure, intent on searching the swim there. From the quay, he could peer into deep water. On its ramp, he halted, snuffling suspiciously, freezing suddenly.

Two men stood on the platform. They were not farmers. They wore dark uniforms and probed the thorn thickets. Lut glared askance at the polder. The line snaked away raggedly. He saw men and dogs shifting. They worked abreast, a sombre wave on the marshland, hacking, prodding. Once in a while, someone shouted, a whistle blasted. Otherwise they came silently, heads bent and eyes intent.

The rain deluged.

'How much farther?' asked the woman.

She sat astern, her hair soused, raw cheeks glistening. She looked different, thought the boatman. His other passenger answered. 'We've made our base at the lock, miss.' She looked younger, the boatman reckoned. The dampness sharpened her strong features. 'Not far now,' said the policeman.

'Damn the rain,' said the woman.

'It won't help, miss.'

The boatman steered without speaking. He scanned the banks, sometimes sweeping by reedbeds, but with slight expectation. The marsh kept its secrets. The outboard drowned the rain's clamour and he spat in the hubbub.

The woman wailed, 'Lord, the trouble! We gave the child too much leeway. He never ought to have slipped us.'

'Easy said,' soothed the policeman; 'with hindsight,' he added.

'All along he deceived us.'

'Kids, miss – some are artful.'

'Yes,' she snapped, 'some are tricky.' Kershaw was right, she thought glumly, the department had faltered. He would tighten the reins now, with justification.

'He's not the first to go missing.'

'I know that,' she said tartly.

The boatman eyed them morosely. The air was liquid. He thought, 'Missing! As well search for a marsh wraith!'

'Will it stop?' asked the woman.

'*This* won't stop,' he said, brooding, 'the sky's full o' water. You'd be lucky if this stopped.' They shot the bridge. He looked back at the river. 'She'll be up,' he predicted. 'By tonight you won't know her. She'll be a blamed torrent.'

'Pray the child's under cover.' The woman hugged her arms grimly.

'Missing!' He said it aloud now.

'Official term,' declared the officer.

'Aye,' the boatman wheezed damply, 'so it may be.'

The woman leaned forward. 'You found him once. . . .'

'Once.' He was touched by her anguish. They swirled past dank withies. Gnarled roots flanked the current, and formidable eddies. 'We had the clue then,' he muttered. 'This time the lad's vanished.'

The man in uniform grunted.

'He was wild,' said the boatman, voice fading. Spume lashed, and through the grey precipitation a skein of geese banked to the saltings. Voices muffled, they glided like spectres, one wing raised then the other, spilling air as they whiffled. More followed, shady squadrons, sails droning. Their soulful creak pierced the weather, then the thrum of rain triumphed. 'Some things are wild,' growled the boatman; 'born wild and they live wild.'

He throttled back.

'And come to harm.' The woman looked away, stiffening.

They nosed in through the murk behind a launch rigged with searchlights. Men were grouped near the lock. Some had maps. As the passengers landed, she turned, her face

entreating. The woman paused, her features hardening.
'Suppose the boy was washed downstream, how far – I
mean. . . .'

'Bar getting snagged? Depends on tides.'

'The sea?'

'Could drift to sea,' he said, 'easy.'

'Yes, well. . . .' She left slowly, saying 'thank you,' and
went to the lock house. The boatman pondered the downpour. For a while he stood soaking before, securing the
vessel, he set off across the marshlands.

Water swilled. Already land drains were gushing, filling
dykes from the innings. Pumps churned and reeds jostled.
Now and then the rain gusted, caught by veering sea breezes,
and bands of light ran the channels. Draughts whirled at
intersections. Here the brown bilge grew choppy while
duckweed rafts scattered. The man cursed, his cap streaming. Where scrubby hedges gave cover, he plodded beside
them. More often the land was open. Dripping reeds were
poor shelter. Drenched, he crossed the great arteries – Five
Watering, Highknock – and lurched to the flood grass.

Fowl and sheep hunched in puddles. He skirted hollows.
At last, the reedy moats threaded, he reached the marsh
church and entered. Hunter stood near the pulpit. 'Didn't
say you were coming.'

'Nor you.'

'Soaked for nothing.' Hunter's brusque tone was edgy.
'You're a sodden mess, fellow!'

'Stream's rising.'

'Well, you've wasted your time,'man. The boy hasn't been
here. Damned urchin!'

'It was a chance.' The boatman glanced at the box-pews.
Their gates were latched, the small stalls bare and eerie. The
emptiness was daunting. His shoulders sagged. 'Can't do
more, then.'

'You could pray,' Hunter muttered, 'if you weren't a
damned heathen.'

'Don't you heathen me, mister.' The other quivered, cold
suddenly. He was grey. 'You blamed sinner!'

'So that's it – a bleak outlook.'

'Rain's set in.'

'The first flood.' Hunter stomped the aisle, snarling. 'Too damned early. A child!' He glared up at the timbers. 'Where's the justice, by heaven? Young rogue had the makings. . . .'

The boatman studied the chancel. The altar boards held him, the wide eye drawn on them. The symbol perturbed him. He had seen the eye somewhere – a startled heron, an old ewe down lambing. But he was not one for churches and thought of the urchin. Hunter was right: it looked bleak.

'Why should he go now?' he wondered. 'He lived for those otters.'

'We should have turned him in, blast it!'

'Betrayed him?'

'He'd be safe, man, for God's sake.'

The boatman shrugged. 'Until he bunked. We might have tamed him between us, but we left it too late.' They stood together, coats dripping, like a couple of sealions. 'That's how it is for us, Hunter – too late now for most things.'

Hunter went to the door. The rain was beating the sedges. 'Like hell,' he said fiercely. 'We can mind the damned otters, take care of them for him. He prayed for that. We can guard the brutes for him.'

'It's too late. They won't survive. Too many banks have been changed, too much cover destroyed. Dredgers, sprays – there's too much against the otters.'

'Then we'll fight it.'

'*You* may,' said the boatman.

'I will,' Hunter told him.

'I'm not taking no orders.'

Lut swam up from the jetty with eager strokes. The rain had stopped but the stream was in spate and its brimming flow thrilled him. A dark night hid the cottage. The one window which glowed seemed remote as a star, glimpsed then gone among the reeds. Clouds were scudding. The otter thrust at the current, against the flotsam of autumn. Leaves and twigs slid around him; the boat tugged her moorings. Like the banks, her hull gurgled, passing on the flood's gossip, the newsy song of the river: 'Upstream, eels are stirring!' Lut climbed the rock.

He called Bugle. It was the night of the run and the fishers would banquet.

From the stone he scanned the water. It clacked and swirled past the boulder. Where the banks curved, ripples jostled, nudging earth from the shoulders, twitching into the darkness. The black lane drove swiftly. He saw no life on its surface, just the husks of shed seeds and a medley of berries, then three prow-waves glimmered. Lut watched the snouts spearing water. Bugle's led from the centre. On each side, a cub followed, almost instantly with him, squirming up with shy greetings. He welcomed their mother.

182

'Soon,' his gleam said, 'we guzzle. Tonight is the eel feast.'

She regarded him dourly. With a flip she ducked under, exploring the current. A small trout darted upstream. A minnow flashed and vanished. The deep shadows were barren and the bitch surfaced, snorting. A mean feast, she considered, unimpressed by Lut's smugness.

'Soon,' he drooled. 'The eels are travelling.' From ponds, ditches and channels. By rills. Through wet hollows. Garbed in silver, rich in fat for the sea trek. Lut plunged, cruising briskly. In a while Bugle joined him, though her style was unhopeful. Trailing bubbles, she twirled in lazy circles. He sped past her, eyes probing. Ears and nose clammed, Lut was ready for action, patrolling intently. The female meandered. Her languid turns mocked his zeal until the first serpent loomed, when she stiffened, eyes glinting.

The eel came dimly. Little light pierced the flow and the fish barely shimmered. It grew uncannily, flexing out of the darkness. And as it came, another glimmered; and a third ghosting presence. Dusky greenness encased them. One came low, near the bottom; one near the bank. The third bored the stream's marrow. As the monsters drew nearer, more silver ghosts followed, pumping over black gardens. It seemed the flood was alive now with sinuous travellers, their wide eyes like portholes. With fierce obsession they sallied, teeming seawards in thousands.

Bugle hung near the surface. Choice confused her and, for a moment, she delayed, then Lut was funnelling past her, curving downwards, and the bitch plunged beside him. The dog skimmed the bottom. Eels were marching both flanks and he broke quickly to starboard, attacking the closest. It fled along a drowned chasm. Streaming weeds clutched the otter and he knifed through dark tendrils, blind until the growth parted. His quarry had slipped him. He banked and climbed. The bitch was grappling. Below, a silver shape scurried. Lut went down, his claws splayed, but the eel twisted through them, threading rocks as Lut harried it.

The depths churned. Lut looped upwards. Gulping air, he plunged back to the engagement. Now a long serpent beckoned, its bright hauberk flashing, and he vectored to seize it. The eel streaked. With a swerve Lut took hold and they whirled, the captive threshing. Bugle surged, her jaws snapping. They fished greedily. Savage instincts impelled them, lured the cubs down to join them. Still the silver fleet ventured onwards. Many eels passed unhindered; others died in wild flurries, or escaped through the sludge raised by violent mud tussles.

That night, as of long since on eel tides, the otters gorged. Lips curled and damp coats bristled fiercely, but the fury was over. Now the growling was formal, mere covetous gloating, for the loot was abundant. Lut stretched, his head tigerish. He was Lord of the Levels, of a fine stream, an eel stream. The cubs guzzled. At such times, their sire awed them – not so large as Fingertaker but nonetheless daunting. The young flinched from him, their jowls greasy. Then, as he fell to his own meal, they stuffed again.

A shadow edged to the flood's rim.

It paused. The water vole snuffled. The stream had entered his tunnel and he breasted the current. Philosophically, he paddled. The flood would drop, the bank dry quickly. He knew the way of the seasons, the tide's seesaw rhythms. Dispossessed while the eels ran, he would be home before the ground froze. Meanwhile, he sought lodgings.

Oaring stoutly, he passed the sated otters. They did not scare him, for the gourmands were harmless while eels could be landed. On the whole they were helpful. They had seen off the rat pack and put flight to Esox. Unlike the rats, they could not broach his burrow. He swam inshore, nose working. An old pollard rose darkly. It had roots in the water and the vole beached among them.

A shoe lay stranded in the crevice, a plimsoll, lined with leaves now. He climbed into the object. Puffing his cheeks, the vole curled up on the soft bed and fell asleep.

The shout came closer.

Hunter paused at the wood's edge. The air was sharp. On the banks the webs of spiders were frosted, and his breath steamed. Acorns fell, raising small spouts of water and ringing cadences. He swung his glasses. Bronzed oaks filled the lenses, then tall rushes – growth the boy had once haunted.

184

Hunter still hoped. He searched the slopes, swinging down to the ferry.

Seagulls followed a tractor. Frost twinkled. Upstream, the great rock was captured; Lut sprawled on the summit. Downstream, mallard shafted. He saw the crone and heard her shout for the third time. A moorhen bickered. He scanned the current. The flow hummed quietly, fish rings trembling, leaves swimming. Hunter waited, his hands cold. He rubbed the stump of his fist until the old woman reached him.

'Hunter. . . .'

Sunbeams gilded the rock now. Below the stone, Bugle floated, her cubs playing near her. Lut joined them. With a bounce he was airborne, curling out from the boulder to flop where the others were swimming. With a kick, he led off in a circle, pursued by his offspring.

'Hunter – *the boy's back!*'

Around the rock the beasts scudded, like some monster of legend, nose to tail, undulating. They whirled and bucketed. Soon the game became leapfrog, broad rings spreading outwards. Wavelets hooped the stone platform. Decorum vanished. Madness ruled – the blithe clown in all otters – and Lut romped with gusto. Falling back beside Bugle, he nudged the sleek female. She bit his neck in affection.

'D'you hear, Hunter? He's turned up at the Hall. Are you listening? The child's back.'

'The urchin?' He scarcely dared to believe her.

The cubs had captured an acorn. Squealing, they juggled the object. Hunter watched, his thoughts distant. Memories stirred. Slowly, the sun warmed his fingers as it had in his boyhood, before his pastimes had coarsened. Then he would lie by the river and observe otters playing. He remembered long summers, the cubs in the sedges.

'The urchin's back?' His eyes had moistened.

'Aye,' the crone said. 'The state of him, Hunter!'

'I'll skin him. . . .'

'Lord, the filth!'

'I'll skin the beggar. What's the scoundrel been up to?'

'Hiding. The child was shot at.'

'*The lad's hurt!*'

185

'Bless you, no; the shot missed him. He's unharmed – in the bath now. I've scrubbed him. He's soaking.'

'In the bath?'

'Pink as a baby.'

'I'll be damned!' Hunter came close to smiling. 'In the bath! By God, I'll drown the young scoundrel – I'll have the ears off him!'

Author's note

According to the best evidence, the initial cause of the tragic decline in Britain's otter population during the late 1950s was the widespread use of the pesticide dieldrin, which contaminated the otter's prey. When dieldrin was banned, surviving otters faced other pressures, notably the destruction of natural cover on waterbanks, and the growing use of such waters for leisure purposes.

Today the otter is protected in British law. But that alone will not bring back these shy and splendid animals. The friends of otters have long worked to this end. The Otter Trust has bred otters and released them experimentally; stoics of the Otter Haven Project strive to protect and renew otter habitats; research into otter behaviour is continuing. In Scottish glens, on the Welsh Marches, on the streams of Tarka country, the Vincent Wildlife Trust's representatives have done valuable work.

Will Lut survive? A short walk across the haunts of the last otter from where I write is a dyke marked on the map as Otter Channel. But our otters have been gone now for two decades. They *could* return. On many waters the otter could swim as he used to swim. It depends on whether enough of us care.

A. R. Lloyd
Kent, 1984